Bodies on the Line

OTHER BOOKS BY THE AUTHOR

NON-FICTION
The Art of Survival, Rocky Shore Books

EDITOR
The Sixties, Wayne State University Press
On Nature's Terms, Texas A&M University Press
Sports in America, Wayne State University Press
The Best of Witness: 1987-2007, Michigan State University Press

Bodies on the Line

SHORT FICTION

Peter Stine

REGENT PRESS
Berkeley, California

[Paperback]
ISBN 10: 1-58790-519-1
ISBN 13: 978-1-58790-519-3

[E-Book]
ISBN 10: 1-58790-520-5
ISBN 13: 978-1-58790-520-9

Library of Congress Control Number: 2019944416

Cover photograph: Mark Steinmetz

Manufactured in the U.S.A.

REGENT PRESS

Berkeley, California

www.regentpress.net

In memory of my parents, Betty and Harold

Contents

Bodies on the Line

Meditation

I move among the faces that I meet
in silent awe, as if staring into deserts
singular deserts in cardboard boxes,
watered by cologne and shaded by hair,
with features protruding from the sand –
stump of nose, gash of mouth, flicking eyelash –
each working with feverish independence,
until the nose is blurred by sand,
the mouth fills with sand,
the eyelash is stalled in sand,
until all is paved over with smooth sand
and stunned into a compassion not my own,
I see the mirage of a human face.

Mark Steinmetz

Angling with my Father

Word spread in the elevators of the condo that sharks had arrived, stretching for two miles along the Florida coast. At this very moment they were driving a school of blues into shore out front. I was visiting my father who had just had heart-bypass surgery. I left him dreaming on the sofa and went down to the beach.

But when I reached the ocean, mingling through the crowd of bathers gathered to watch, I found myself standing next to my father. His chest was smooth as new skin. A distant freighter balanced like a toy on the horizon. As we looked out to sea, I felt my spirits rise, for my father's stapled saw-toothed scar, which I had nursed with ointment for days, had taken up residence in the busy mouths of sharks.

They were beside themselves with opportunity, a magnified spectacle. The blues were being driven in closer and closer to us. As waves rose to breaking, forming a sudden aquarium, shark shadows darted like torpedoes through the momentary wall of sparkling water and struck the blues, sending up blossoms of red. Inside the breakers, fins motored through the bubbling white foam, for scores of blues were now trapped in the shallows.

My father stood beside me with a fishing pole. He cast his line far out over the breakers, but with each cast, it was the sharks that struck the bait, not the blues. Each time the line was broken, the rod went straight, and each time my father reeled in the line, only to try again.

Then hysteria broke out before our eyes. The blues were leaving their world, swimming in and trying to beach themselves on the wet sand, only to be drawn back by the undertow. I waded into the surf. The temperature of the ocean was warm with massacre. If I could grab a blue by the tail and toss it up onto the sand behind me, away from the sharks, nosing in this shimmering silver pool of scales, my father and I were free.

I looked to my right. A young man in Bermuda shorts was advancing up the beach. He had a blue by the tail, its head missing, torn off at the gills.

That afternoon I fished with my hands. I remember my father had told me that blues were good eating. I felt their bodies thrashing and tails slapping at my ankles. I looked into the eyes of sharks, saw their tiny brains work the instant before they made up their minds. Soon I had a small catch of blues dying on the sand behind me, gills gaping for air, opening and closing in a kind of gratitude. My hands were scraped raw with the labor. My arms ached as if removing the blues from the ocean was a deep violation of gravity.

I lost track of my father.

Later when I returned to the condo, up the elevator, past open doorways where the sounds of television eclipsed the roar of the surf out front, my father was still dreaming on the sofa.

The Diplomat

He was recently divorced, out of work in Detroit, collecting unemployment, and making some extra money under the table ghostwriting testimonials for a weight-loss clinic. This hardly qualified him for a diplomatic post at the United Nations, but that's what occurred. He would learn some years later the offer was rescue work, set in motion by a former classmate at Amherst, upon learning that his future had stalled. He jumped at the opportunity as if summoned to a new and complex fate.

He flew to New York above a cover of clouds, just pure sunshine and infinite blue. His mind was willfully blank. A blue taxi drove him from LaGuardia into Manhattan, pulling up at the United Nations building on First Avenue and Forty-Fifth Street. He took an elevator to the fortieth floor, in time to join a group of diplomats at a morning session on economic growth. He had been instructed to meet his American contact here. Manhattan, with its honking traffic, its ethnic coleslaw of pedestrians, flowed on far below. Gathered in the room were men of various races, most of them stout, dressed in tribal robes and military tunics as well as expensive suits. He stayed as inconspicuous as possible as they moved comfortably around glass tables filled with pastries and coffee urns. It seemed logical that for these diplomats, most of them representing very impoverished nations, weight was distinction.

A crew-cut American official appeared, and framed against a plate-glass window, introduced him as a newly appointed U.S. delegate who was an authority on world hunger. He looked behind him for such a person, since his last job was not to alleviate hunger but exploit it through scams. The smell of toothpaste and cologne filled the air, making him feel dizzy, and he sank into a nearby couch, but not before saying to the blur of faces, "Let's be clear about one thing. I am no expert on world hunger." But this candor only made the diplomats more ready, even eager to come over and shake his hand, smiling as if in amiable recognition of the raw realities and duplicity that bound them all together.

He already knew the raw realities of their politics back home: economic need, loss of human rights, arbitrary arrests, torture, death squads, even genocide. Weight loss was not an issue. He imagined some of these diplomats were working to eradicate these problems, while others spoke for regimes probably guilty of perpetrating them. He made a resolution to avoid quick moral judgment. That first week he embraced his role as an *ersatz* authority on world hunger, reading up on the subject at night in the single room he had rented in the East Village.

A routine developed. He would emerge from the morning subway and once high in the United Nations building, hold counsel with diplomats at various sessions, often having lunch with them in a cafeteria overlooking the East River. He even befriended a diplomat his own age from Uzbekistan, a nation with a terrible human rights record. Handsome, with a full mustache, he spoke perfect English and wore a military tunic with red epaulets. The Uzbek was a former racing cyclist, with a wife and young daughter now, and spoke with excitement of his adventures abroad. He rode his bike around Manhattan, and told the American that biking the roads of his home city of Andijan was dangerous because of IEDs, either planted by Islamic terrorists or the government trying to frame them.

In general, the new diplomat's contact with others from so many different nations pleased him. Up close they seemed just men, most likely with wives and families, more survivors than transgressors. Maybe all their sonorous talk of progress and justice expressed a desire, however throttled or compromised, to reduce the suffering in their countries. No different in a way from the false testimonials he had dreamed up to inspire the obese.

After a month at the United Nations, now boosted by the vision of a real community of nations, he decided to invite a group of diplomats to a hockey game in Madison Square Garden. They were led to seats down next to the ice, behind one goal, virtually in the midst of the smooth slashing skates and colliding bodies. No protective plate-glass shield separated them from the action. As the game progressed, he watched his guests become more absorbed. A tiny enclave of murmuring foreign tongues in an arena that expanded with rhythmical roars as players swept up and down the ice, attacking or retreating from the goal like the flapping of some enormous wing.

The last period featured a rally, interrupted by a fight between a Ranger and Penguin player, punching and tugging at each other like lobsters standing on their tails. The crowd was frenzied, and in the fading moments a Ranger slap shot was fired directly on goal in front of them. A roar erupted as eyes in the arena awaited the flash of the red light behind the net. Instead silence fell, as attention turned to a figure in a military tunic lying face down behind the goal. The errant puck had struck his friend from Uzbekistan. Immediately he leaped over the sideboards and was kneeling beside him. One arm looked unhinged, reaching over his head at an impossible angle, while the other lay in a splayed position, like a broken doll. Blood spread from under his tunic and his mouth into the ice. Standing up under the floodlights, the American diplomat stared into the upper tier of seats as the Garden came alive again, in a surge of what felt like patriotic pride, a glacial rumble of stamping feet that shook the very foundation of the arena.

Memorial

The girl always seemed to be there. No visible connection to anyone at all. Maybe nine or ten, with blond pigtails and wearing a plain calico dress, she stood beneath the statue of a Civil War soldier on the village green. As if she were keeping him company, as one should at a memorial. People walking by would notice her or not, but her blue eyes, when not distracted by birds frolicking in a nearby tree or kids playing at the far edge of the green, were focused on the soldier.

A young policeman had noticed her several times that weekend, through the open window of his squad car while driving by the green. Whether she was there at night or not he was not on duty to check. However, on Sunday it was raining hard and she was still there, huddled at the granite base of the statue, soaked and shivering, yet as anchored to the earth as the memorial itself.

This was not right and the policeman got out of the squad car and walked over. Reaching the girl, he squatted down so they were on the same eye level. Looking into her freckled face he was instantly disoriented, uncertain, as if he could not find his own reflection in an empty mirror. To regain mental balance, he stared straight upward, tracing the rifle leaning against the tattered military coat of the soldier, then up to his face, the thick mustache, the grey-white eyes, the overall impression of iron will and unspeakable memory.

She was silent, her hands hugging her elbows.

"Are your parents around?"

"That's my father," she said proudly, gazing up at the statue.

The policeman stood up and read the inscription on the memorial. No specific name, but the soldier represented a Michigan regiment from the area lost at the Battle of Antietam in 1863, information he had never bothered to notice before.

"Listen," he said, turning back to the girl, "can I give you a ride home?"

She stared at him.

"Well, at least let me get you out of the rain."

The girl offered him her hand and they walked to the squad car. He found a thick terrycloth towel in the trunk and wrapped it around her, then put her in the passenger seat and drove to the police station, a red brick building at the far corner of the four-block downtown.

He led her into an office off the lobby of the station and another officer brought in some hot cocoa and left.

"Now tell me, do your parents live in town? I can call

them to come and take you home."

"You forgot. My father was killed in the Civil War. He didn't look like that statue when he died. He was lying in a ditch next to two other soldiers and his eyes were wide open and staring at the sky."

"How do you know this?"

"I read about Antietam in a book, but my father I see every night when I fall asleep. In the daytime I stay by his statue because it looks almost alive, even though it isn't."

"You wait here. I'll be right back."

The policeman left and went back into the lobby where a heavy-set, bearded officer was reading a magazine at the front desk.

"John, we need a doctor over here quick. That little girl I brought in is delusional, or worse. She's lost, won't give me her name or address. She thinks that her father is the Civil War statue over on the green."

"Well," the officer drawled, "that counts as a major delusion all right. At least somebody noticed the memorial. I'll call up Stevenson right now."

The policeman, who had a daughter of his own at home, returned to the girl in his office. She had put aside the towel, and he couldn't help but be taken by her loveliness, the way her hair, no longer in pigtails, had dried into golden ringlets. That disorientation he had experienced on the green returned, and when she started speaking he saw that everything she had said earlier and was telling him

14

now was true. How all her many brothers had been casualties of war. With stunning precision she evoked their images in his mind. One drowned in a shell crater outside Belleau Woods, one entangled with a dead German soldier in the Ardennes, one frozen to death in a bunker on Heartbreak Ridge, one face down in the mud of Khe Sanh, one unrecognizably charred in the wreckage of a Humvee in Fallujah.

She stopped speaking with a cryptic smile on her face. The policeman was bent over in his chair, hands at his temples, unable to understand what was happening.

"McLain," said a voice at the door, "Stevenson's here."

He stood up and went unsteadily into the lobby. When he returned with the doctor, the girl was gone. At once the police conducted a search of the town and surrounding area. But no one of her description, provided with poetic accuracy by the policeman, was ever found. Over the next few days, on his rounds in the squad car, the policeman passed by the green and saw what appeared to be a ghostly outline of the girl still standing at the memorial. Then his mental balance returned, and soon moments like that ceased altogether.

Luxury Suite

Jocks at Wayne State were now hanging around my office in State Hall to get a glimpse of the gastric oracle. Neurologists and dieticians at UM hospitals contacted me, inviting my participation in medical research programs. Women were trying to contact me on Match.com, even though the only photo on my profile page was my yellow Lab. I got letters and emails from strangers asking if I could help them recover money or lost relatives. The Chicago Bears, our chief rival in the NFL, called to offer me a six-week, expense-paid trip to the Bahamas sponsored by Weight Watchers. But in the main I found celebrity status overrated. And did the world really need another fly-by-night charlatan making apocryphal statements about everything? Plus, I had my own issues to worry about: obesity and growing depression.

It all started three months ago when the executive manager of the Detroit Lions learned from his son, a student of mine at Wayne State, that I could affect the fortunes of the team by the amount of food I ate watching their games. I didn't know how or why I had acquired this power. At first I brushed it off it as coincidence. After all, any one of thousands of Lions fans, all pigging out while watching a game, could just as easily and with equal legitimacy take credit for a win. I was Scottish and knew my David Hume: constant conjunction is not causal connection.

Apparently wanting to check me out, Rick's father invited the two of us to his mansion in Palmer Woods for a meal during a Lions game. James greeted us at the front door, wearing a Hawaiian-blue sports jacket that went with his silver-gray hair. It was amazing how people were drawn into absurd ways of thinking, especially when looking for hope. Rick and I sank into a leather couch, facing a flat-screen TV that covered an entire mahogany wall. Before us was a long coffee table loaded with platters of food – tortillas, chips and guacamole dip, cheesecake, cinnamon rolls, stuffed mushrooms, Chicken Kiev. Everything was professionally prepared. Before the kickoff James paced around the den, inviting me to dig in. By now I was starting to feel like a guinea pig in some lab experiment.

The Lions were playing the Steelers that Sunday and fell behind early. Any attempt at a comeback was snuffed out by mind-numbing penalties, which had marked the team for decades. James watched from a far couch, saying nothing. But at halftime he broke out some marijuana, which surprised me given his position with the Lions. I accepted a joint. Rick seemed embarrassed by the scene, wandering nervously in and out of the den. The marijuana was strong, and lifted me above the literal weirdness of the moment. Soon enough I was nibbling on stuffed mushrooms, some Chicken Kiev, then a platter of cornbread on the coffee table. The Lions started to close the gap.

Rick brought in more food for the fourth quarter – sirloin strips, giant shrimp, lobster, and king crab with supreme sauce. Although filled up, I was still high enough to graze on these selections. The game was winding down on the giant screen. The Steelers had the lead, but turned the ball over deep in Lion territory. We took possession at the two-minute warning, down by seven points.

James cleared his throat. "Ken, if you are willing, I'd like to conduct an experiment. Rick has told me about this ability of yours regarding the Lions. Do you mind?"

"I owe you that much just for your hospitality."

James sat next to me on the couch as the Lions began their last drive. Stafford was third-and-long when I was handed a giant lobster tail that I began gnawing on. The Lions converted. On the next series a Bush fumble appeared to end the rally, until it was erased by a Steeler penalty while I was finishing off the sirloin strips. I was completely stuffed, but James kept pushing food at me as the Lions advanced down the field. As time was running out, cheesecake poised at my lips, Johnson made a spectacular leap in the end zone for a score that left the Lions trailing by a point.

"This is amazing," James said softly, rubbing his temples.

"They're going for two!" Rick exclaimed from the doorway,

As Stafford stood over center, I picked up two bacon-and-peanut-butter crackers on the coffee table, very large ones, and bolted them down. Stafford converted on a quarterback sneak. The Lions won in what could only be called miraculous fashion. James abruptly left the room without a word. I left a few minutes later, Rick standing at the front door, eyes averted.

When I got back to my apartment in Sherwood Forest, Jill was waiting on the front porch. She was attractive and smart, with shining black hair cropped like Prince Valiant. She found me different from other academics she had met. Most of them, she assured me, were just smart enough to be real pricks. She said I was the more puzzling, bohemian sort. We had been seeing each other for about a year.

I couldn't resist telling her about what happened in Palmer Woods. She listened, and then laughed. "Maybe you should go with this new power of yours, Ken. I hear the Lions need some kind of divine intervention. But just don't overdo it. I like that lean body of yours." Whatever else, our relationship was sexual. Later that night, Jill was pressing her body so completely into mine I didn't know which was which.

The next week James contacted me. Expecting to be denied tenure at Wayne State, I accepted his offer of the improbable job of sitting in a luxury suite at Ford Field and, essentially, eating the Lions to victory. And from the start I did my job well, though with a price to pay for my exorbitant desire to please. After each game, you could find me bent over the bumper of my Ford Focus in the parking lot and vomiting my payload onto the pavement. But the Lions went on a winning streak that lasted the rest of the season, snapped only by my absence from the suite for one game when my doctor ordered me to fast a week to relieve a bloated stomach. Over those two months I had gained a lot of weight. It had already cost me my lovely girlfriend, who had taken up with a triathlon runner.

The *Detroit Free Press* sent out a reporter to interview me and the story appeared on the front page of the Sports section. My career as a celebrity was launched. I received a flood of letters from Lions fans, most expressing gratitude for my unusual contribution to the team's success. Many confided that their obesity was brought on by a compulsive need to snack while watching sports on TV. They asked me for advice, not realizing I was the problem. A Baptist pastor downtown invited me to address his congregation, saying that anyone watching the Lions this season was "bearin' witness to a Resurrection!" I thanked him, but with no faith to speak of, had to decline. Local Channel 4 News interviewed me, and I surprised some viewers in taking a degree of blame for the obesity epidemic, setting a bad example for multitudes of fans. These people had become easier to understand, worthy of sympathy because I was now one of them. While I ate for the money, I envisioned millions more across the country eating themselves sick because those shirt-staining calories were at least one reliable source of sensory experience in their lives. I felt guilty, too. Unless the opponents of the Lions had found some duplicate of me willing to eat his way into oblivion, canceling me out so to speak, as things stood this was plain cheating. I would have preferred teaching a class on the role of survivor guilt in the novels of Ernest Hemingway. Instead I was fixing professional football games with the help of a fluky faculty I still couldn't account for.

I had been a toned athlete three months ago, but with two weeks left in the season had ballooned up so much I needed help getting around. My hand didn't fit into the garbage disposal to retrieve a soda cap. I constantly needed a new set of clothes to squeeze into. Doorways were a challenge, often impassable. Now an elevator took me up to the luxury suite at Ford Field, a man with a wheelchair waiting when the door slid open. I was gripped more and more by a craving to eat that had nothing to do with any football game. There was a mysterious acceleration of my obesity, out of all proportion to the amount of food I was shoveling in, which was plenty – enough to get the Lions into the playoffs, something they had not achieved in decades.

What had earned me money and almost mythical status in Detroit, bolting down food, was threatening to devour me. Those last two weeks I stuck to business. I was cognizant of how often the TV monitor hanging above my head in the suite revealed that cameras were focused on me, hunkered down, and lost in the window glare, laboring to breathe while sticking mozzarella sticks between my cheeks.

By the time the playoffs started, I was hosting a ten-minute pre-game telecast in the luxury suite, where regular fans could come and interview me. It was a humbling experience. I found these people to be impressive, knowledgeable about football, worried about their families and jobs, deeply stoical. Their enthusiasm for the Lions seemed a half-conscious bid to regain a sense of community, something long absent from their lives. Their addiction to sports talk, both on radio and with each other, even in the suite, served as a surrogate for democratic debate in a country whose politicians had not the slightest interest in their opinions. Obesity was the heartless triumph of the fast food industry over individual will. No one wanted to be fat. Economic inequality impoverished their lives in ways the mainstream media made sure they never fully grasped. But I was an intellectual, and their quirky, insightful take on so many things cheered me up for reasons I would never understand.

The suite was packed during these telecasts. The producer had me seated on an elevated platform in the kitchen area, 390 pounds of flesh on display, in colorful clothes, of course, but not an edifying sight. Fans were incredulous when I told them that my feet, now hidden from my view beneath a bulging stomach and thunderous thighs, were the same feet that had sped me to the Michigan Class B high school medley relay championship eighteen years ago. I felt embarrassed, exposed, but they treated me with a kind of sanctity, as if my physical condition were some voluntary crucifixion that I was enduring for their sake. After the last telecast I was touched when a short, gray-haired man, a retired physician, leveled with me, warning that the obesity I was assuming to bolster the Lions was endangering my life.

The Lions marched through the playoffs and the city was euphoric. Stories about me appeared everywhere. Even *USA Today* and several cable sports programs were paying attention. But while the Lions rested during the off-week before the Super Bowl, I was a wheezing orb of flesh, hardly able to move, unless rolling. That retired physician was right. I had to choose whether to live or die.

I requested James visit me two days before the Lions would meet the New England Patriots. Jill, long absent from my life, was replaced now by a broad nurse who munched jellybeans while helping me move around the apartment. She always carried a blood-pressure kit whose belt wasn't long enough to encircle my upper arm.

James sat in my living room inspecting me. He looked

optimistic. If appalled by my condition, he didn't show it. Probably he wasn't appalled at all, since how I looked at the moment was consistent with, indeed necessary for the Lions to have come this far.

"How're you feeling, Ken? I hear you're having some health issues . . . But you've taken us to the Super Bowl! I still can't believe it."

"James. I'm dying."

"You've given hope to the people of Detroit, a hard-luck city!"

I repeated what I said.

He hesitated. "Just one more game, Ken, one more. It's the Super Bowl."

"I quit, James."

The Lions lost the Super Bowl. I was relieved the game was competitive and that I played no role in the outcome. I had no further contact with the organization either. It was apparent the Lions would sacrifice any fan, even one possessed with putative supernatural powers, to achieve success. My notoriety faded quickly. Because the season had ended in defeat, the sports media couldn't resist placing some of the blame on me. The *Detroit Free Press* ran a mocking headline in its post-game coverage, declaring that the Lions missed winning the Super Bowl by "a pork chop."

I returned to my Zen practice and some serious fasting. Soon I started jogging long distances through Palmer

Park, then exercising every day at the Y. Within four months I was back to 175 pounds. I was rereading Marcus Aurelius' *Meditations*. My brush with the supernatural had only deepened my distrust of all things religious.

Then I ran into Jill at the Y. She looked dazzling in a black leotard. All I believed in now was this sort of good luck. I suggested we get together so I could fill her in on a celebrity whose star had exploded. I told her that I was out of work, collecting unemployment, and earning a little extra at a weight-loss clinic peddling diet candy bars that caused gas.

She agreed to go jogging with me. Then things got better.

Bus Ride

Once Lenore got on the bus and purchased a ticket, she glanced up the aisle and recognized the man who last Saturday night had forced her behind an apartment with a knife to her throat and raped her. He was seated in the back, with a baseball cap pulled down over his eyes. Reading a newspaper, he didn't notice her. She knew he was the one by the straw-colored hair and that cauliflower right ear, which she had stared at through shock and pain as he was thrusting into her. He had placed the knife on the ground and she remembered thinking she could reach it with her hand. It wasn't lack of courage that prevented her but something else. Violence as an act of self-defense or revenge was not a possibility she could even imagine. How does one stab someone? She had walked back to her apartment sobbing, and after a phone call a policeman came to the door to get information about the assault. Young and polite, with close-cropped hair, he assured her that she was lucky to have escaped further violence. The knife might have come into play. Whether this was said to make her feel better or not she wasn't sure. She had been silent and passive during the rape, as if utterly dispossessed of her own body, and wondered when the policeman left whether that had saved her life or made her a perfect victim.

She took a seat across from the driver's booth. Her insides were melting and she felt moisture on her brow. It was as if she were being forced to experience the rape over again. The foreign smell of his neck, the weight of his forearms pressing down on her, it all came back. Any option of doing something on the bus was far beyond her reach, and she turned her face to look out the window. A straggling line of kindergarten kids filled the sidewalk across the street, linked to each other by a security rope. Then the bus pulled back onto its route, and several blocks later the brakes hissed again, jolting passengers forward as it came to a stop,

Suddenly he was standing in the aisle, preparing to get off and staring down on her. "Excuse me, ma'am, you got an extra quarter so I can catch another bus to get back home? Can you help me out?" She looked up at him. The huge body, grizzled chin, blue eyes sparkling out of two slits. That ear. But he didn't recognize her. Even though she would never forget him, she was gone from his memory. She hesitated, then an involuntary reflex kicked in and she handed him a quarter. "Thank you, ma'am." Her hatred for him was matched only by fear and shame at her capitulation.

When the bus was moving again, Lenore was so

overwhelmed by the vision of a world filled with rapists, inescapable, that she failed to notice her regular neighborhood stop had come and gone. She ignored the next stop, her delicate face now hard and blank as stone. She knew what to do. She would ride the bus route again and make an investigation. At every stop through town, then back through the residential neighborhoods, when a man climbed on the bus she recognized a rapist. The business executive with the brown pin-stripped suit and razor-cut hair. The black teenager with the tattooed biceps and low-slung jeans. Then the young priest with a yellow stain on his clerical collar. The muscular jarhead with the paranoid eyes and camouflage fatigues. Finally the mechanic with gray flecks in his hair and grease stains on his blue work shirt. She marveled how they came in such variety, how their mask of innocence was so perfect. What could a woman do?

When she reached her apartment she was flushed and nauseous. Her black Lab was anxious, came over to rest his head on her lap, but she was not distracted. Certainly the bus was no longer a safe mode of transportation. There was always her bike, but it needed a new chain, was useless in bad weather or for shopping. She had no single friend, no acquaintance she could think of who might be drafted as a bodyguard. She recognized that such thoughts that presumed her permanent vulnerability led nowhere. But for now she would allow them to run their course, like images projected on a distant drive-in movie screen.

Then Lenore remembered that bulletin in the local newspaper about a women's self-defense class being offered at the YMCA in her neighborhood. Maybe she should sign up. That evening she walked to the building, but to reach the registration counter she had to pass through an area filled with nautilus machines and weightlifting equipment. She flinched. All about her were scantily clad men challenging the force of gravity, their muscles bulging, breathing hard. Rapists in training. For a moment she grew dizzy and staggered a little, but clinging to the idea of self-defense she moved forward. Quietly she asked the teenage girl working at the counter for a program of activities. A faint thrill traversed through her as she leafed through its pages, searching for an advanced class for women interested in training with knives.

Wrecks

Lane awoke to a squeal, a thud, and then a second whoosh of metal collapsing into metal. There were no screams. His bedroom window was gaping open, a breeze fluttering the curtains. From the basement a water heater clanked like some enraged pulse from the next world. He rolled out of bed and pulled on his pants, put in contacts, and went out front.

The Datsun was still untouched. Dented, the battery dead, the car squatted in a puddle at the curb, its high fenders, like mini-skirts, exposing the drollery of sagging and rusted private parts.

A small group of neighbors had gathered across the street in Tyrone's front yard, surveying the wreckage. His new blue Volkswagen bug was smashed up against a tree at the curb, and his new red Volkswagen van, still parked in the driveway, had its entire right side caved in. A rusted maroon Nova now rested in the middle of the yard between the two wrecks like a giant lawn ornament. The driver and his companion remained sitting in the front seat in a cloud of disconnections. It was easy enough to connect the dots.

The Nova must have come down Canterbury, missed the turn at Piccadilly, hit the bug, veered around the tree, tearing up roots and sod, and then ploughed into the van. Lane crossed the street. His neighbor could not be living right with two new cars all but demolished by some junk-bucket speeding through the neighborhood early on a Sunday morning. But the loss was only material, and he allowed himself that sly sense of relief, even pleasure, to be found in another's misfortunes. Except for Tyrone's heavy-set wife Lorraine, in curlers and terrycloth bathrobe, now surveying the damage from her front porch, he was the only white person around.

A huge panda-shaped man, Tyrone was dressed in starched combat fatigues and sported an Afro that sprang from his caramel-colored head like a thousand exclamation marks. He was bent over and peered into the Nova, conversing with its two occupants. He acted embarrassed, indeed apologetic about the inconvenience this might be causing them.

"You brothers all right?" he asked. As the driver climbed out of the Nova, Jim and Sophia came over from next door. Jim was a bright Harvard-educated lawyer working for the mayor downtown and had a pad out, scribbling notes.

"Naw, I ain't hurt–" came the slurred reply. The driver was tall, maybe in his mid-twenties, wearing a soiled white T-shirt and a Tigers cap perched back on his head. He reeked of booze and ghetto poverty. "This wasn't as bad as the last one we was in," he said to himself. "Los' the roof o' that car."

Suddenly a long arm appeared from the passenger side window and carefully stood a bottle of White Label scotch whiskey on the roof of the Nova.

A squad car pulled up to the curb and two white policemen, youthful and clean-cut, got out and walked over toward the gathering. Quickly Tyrone came forward to intercept them. "We got things here under control," he snapped. "We don't need you harassing the brothers."

Lorraine didn't appreciate the scripted solidarity. "Tyrone, come over here!" she barked. Her husband retreated halfway to the porch.

The policemen remained cool and efficient. "Is this your car?" one asked the driver.

A pair of blood-shot eyes stared at nothing. "I guess tha' right."

"So what happened?"

"Nothin'. We was just rappin'. We both got kids, officer. We wasn't out tryin' to get laid or anything. We wasn't into marijuana or anything like that. We was just out lookin' for a career–"

"Listen to him lie," Sophia said under her breath. She had the broad, stern, intelligent face of a committed urban schoolteacher. Jim continued to take notes.

"What about the liquor bottle?" the policeman asked.

"We was drinkin' earlier with my sister, but we wasn't

drunk." He blinked several times as it dawned on him that his car, headlights shattered, was parked on a stranger's front lawn. "We wasn't tryin' to cause no trouble. I hope this thing don't turn into what it might turn into." His eyes wandered toward Tyrone for support. "I don't want this to get *political*–"

The second policeman returned from a stroll up the sidewalk. "What about those skid marks back at the stop sign?"

"Nope, none of those marks was made by my car. I was goin' only thirty, maybe thirty-five. If the speed limit around here is twenty-five maybe I was doin' that. I don't know – I wasn't lookin' what speed, tell you the truth. I was lightin' a cigarette. I don't know this neighborhood, never been down this street. These streets are curvy, like they was in the mountains."

Lane stared down Canterbury to check.

Tyrone had now transformed into an entirely different person, anxious and practical, huddling with Jim as he scribbled on his pad. Maybe it dawned on him that he was out two cars thanks to these "brothers" and had better get the facts straight for any future insurance claims. Lane felt some sympathy for him. Surely Tyrone's political posturing was common enough among middle-class blacks in Detroit. Drifting back across the street, he watched Tyrone all that morning out in his front yard, dejectedly circling his two wrecked cars, brand new all right but now still as corpses. It was as if inspecting them closely enough might somehow help him understand and accept things, maybe bring them back to life.

That afternoon Lane sat on the living room floor, listening through the torn screen door to robins chirping and the drowsy sound of lawn mowers. But the water heater started up again. On the upstairs landing a few white garbage bags were poised, ready to plunge down the stairwell. In the kitchen was a refrigerator, huge and white, laying on its side, exhaling a last few carious breaths.

Wreckage wherever you looked: giant white sperm of possessions, strange, dead, in another week a headache.

He had to change his life. It was obvious. Three weeks ago their cat Carter had disappeared, gone out in search of Jennifer, who had fled to California for a month. She sent him a tape with a recording of her voice repeating over and again: "Here Carter . . . Here kitty, here Carter . . ." He had walked through the neighborhood with the tape recorder hung around his neck at high volume, for hours, day and night. The neighbors listened to her voice too, wondering once again about this strange white couple. But it worked. A week later Carter appeared on the back porch, his gray fur matted and bristled, dirt-caked, looking like a black tumbleweed. Maybe Jennifer would now read his mind and send a tape summoning him back.

Finally he arose and went upstairs to play the flute.

At the heart of his melody was a vision. It was as if Tyrone had folded away his combat fatigues and reappeared with a legion of avenging municipal angels. All Lane's possessions are lined up at the curb as the stricken garbage collectors arrive at dawn. There's a huddle of conspiracy. Rags are dipped into a pail of kerosene, stuffed into a bottle. Reeking black hands light the fuse, a straight-armed lob, then an explosion. They screech off in a giant white truck.

Invisibility

Kyle was born kind. When he was eight and the family lived in Topeka, a man in rags appeared on the front porch selling rotten bananas from a burlap bag. The boy stared through the screen door, recoiling at the halitosis. Then his mother appeared behind him and told the man they didn't need any bananas. She didn't understand he needed to sell them to live. Kyle would never forget him dragging that filthy bag down the street.

When the family moved outside Boston, the boy became aware of a retarded man with a bad stutter living across the street with his mother. Every Monday Ralphy would be standing at the back door asking for permission to drag the trashcans to the curb, where they already stood. When Kyle explained this to him, the grizzled face registered surprise, then confusion. "Okay . . . Gotta cigaweet?"

"I'm sorry, Ralphy, but my parents don't smoke."

"Well, I be goddamned!"

The figure would wander back across the street, only to show up the next week with the same request. Kyle wondered if he had forgotten over the course of seven days that no one in the house smoked. The neighbors were amused, but having to disappoint someone like Ralphy, week after week, made him feel like he was being crucified.

And there was Zoot, a six-foot-four black student in his middle-school class in Atlanta. The school had held him back for years, serving as a holding cell until he turned sixteen and was allowed to disappear. He slept undisturbed in the back row of the classroom, except when Miss Douglas, the history teacher, snuck back and sprayed him with perfume. It was Kyle's job to wake him up after recess each day, where he was usually lying outside under some tree. When the giant accidentally bumped into him when he was bent over a drinking fountain, bloodying his lip, Kyle stood there stunned as the principal arrived to lead Zoot away. Two years later, waiting to catch a bus for high school, a friend poked him in the ribs with a rolled-up copy of the *Miami Herald*. There on the front page was Zoot, flanked by two policemen, arrested for killing a woman in Florida with an ice pick.

Kyle didn't mistake his resurgent kindness for any sort of innate virtue. It was instantaneous, a hardwired reflex. When he was twelve, he had come upon an old hardcover edition of *All Quiet on the Western Front* and read every word. That led to his pouring over books of black-and-white photographs of the trenches. Young men, bodies mutilated, rotting in mud, crusted with snow, ultimately ten million dead, a third of them rendered invisible, blown to bits by bombs and artillery. This changed his vision of reality, and he would move forward in life dismissing personal happiness as a kind of trivial pursuit. He joined thousands of his generation in support of the civil rights movement and opposition to the war in Vietnam.

But matters took a more peculiar turn in his relations with women. He saw his opposite as a primary attraction. Someone without his luck and privilege, whose insecurities, even misfortunes, made her more interesting. Here at least was an opportunity for rescue. The neediness was the appeal.

Kyle was teaching philosophy at the University of Michigan when he met her over the Internet. Jane was thirty-eight, attractive, volatile, her confrontational style belied by sleek auburn hair and a lovely smile. A pregnant runaway at seventeen, she gave her baby up for adoption in NYC and then fled to California to work as a topless waitress in North Beach. She had many bizarre affairs, countless miscellaneous jobs, all terminated by flare-ups with her bosses. Her defiance had no cause. She returned to NYC where she sold jewelry she made off a blanket where the ferry crossing the East River docked for passengers. Later she launched a successful business selling art to corporate clients. She hired a detective to find her daughter but without success. Her stories of survival and gutsy self-reliance intrigued him. Kyle only needed to imagine the chaos of her life, without parents or any guidance, to create an existential heroine.

Jane sensed his kindness, suspension of judgment, and so clung to him. The sex was good, she leading the way, but she demanded an hour of cuddling afterwards, as if nursing some wound suffered long before Kyle appeared, but which he was expected to remedy. But wasn't this brand of empathy leading him off track? He was unable to relax with his circle of Ann Arbor friends, people he had known for years. Jane found them objectionable – too morally righteous, too obsessed with art, too caring of animals, too intellectual, and more likely too much a distraction from Kyle's focus on her. She was always tugging him into mutual invisibility.

She never linked his social presence, bordering on absence, to her presence. It was her insecurity and aloneness that arrested him at these parties, and he would usually end up agreeing with her complaints. Almost as an afterthought, he saw that her judgments were becoming his own, seizing control, whittling down his identity.

Whatever Jane wanted to do in the summer they did. She urged him to get a bike, since cycling had been a pastime of hers for years. Kyle was a good athlete and took to the challenge. She was faster on the road and he always trailed behind. They took a bike tour down the east coast of Lake Champlain and through northern Vermont. A few days out, Jane quarreled with the tour leader, and at breakfast the next day insisted the two of them move to a separate table away from the others. Near the end of the tour, cycling through a small village, he collided with an elderly man crossing the street. Obviously he had not been seen. The last day he lagged unnoticed behind the last tour guide on the road, and caught a lift in the security van that was trailing the cyclists into Middlebury.

Kyle's instincts grew more wary of giving offense. He didn't blame Jane. He had a history of standing up to those who didn't treat others or himself with respect. But that self had checked out. Even Jane had urged him to summon back the person she had fallen for. "Stand up for yourself!" she urged, even though she realized he might take her advice and walk away. But he deferred to a vast ocean of loneliness he saw awaiting her.

One morning, brushing his teeth, Kyle looked up to find the bathroom mirror reflected only a toothbrush moving back and forth in the air and the shower curtain behind. There was no sign of his body. Poking his ribs where they had been, he felt something solid and bony in what the mirror told him was empty space. He moved into the bedroom, lay down on the crumpled sheets, and closed his eyes. When he opened them, he could see bare feet and wiggling toes. He was relieved, but still couldn't fathom what had just happened. The link with Jane's domination of him seemed both obvious and absurd.

He brought the matter up with his psychotherapist. He always felt he had to deliver a problem for each session, like throwing a fish up on the dock, and this one was a whopper. His psychotherapist was smart and sympathetic, knew very well his history with Jane. Kyle told him about turning invisible before the mirror. "What's happening, Mark? Should I see a brain neurologist? Am I suffering from some new syndrome?"

Mark looked at him, smiling, stroking his beard with long fingers. "Disappearing in a physical sense is an act of choice, Kyle. It's something, as you know, I have advised you try with Jane. But what you're describing today is a mystery to me. Unless you're hallucinating."

He knew nothing was so difficult as not deceiving yourself, but ventured forth: "I think it's Jane's influence on me. Something weird is happening. I mean lately the two of us have been waking up to analyze the same dreams."

The bouts of invisibility started to come more regularly, lasting for just an instant, but still alarming. Kyle would throw a ball across an open field for his Lab to retrieve, but then, with ball in mouth, the dog would just stand there, looking around, not knowing where to return. He'd be reading on his front porch when neighbors walked by, without offering a greeting or even glance. At the Y some obese man almost sat on him when he was sweating in the sauna. He read up on invisibility and was not reassured. Most things were invisible anyway, just infinite space between atoms.

But physics was not his problem. Sacrificing what he wanted for what Jane wanted released him from pursuing his own aims, which grew more unclear the longer he neglected them. That he might be rescuing her by simply being present in her life was too self-flattering to be considered. Yet invisibility did have its appeal. It was the physical equivalent of selflessness. Jane sensed this, and grew exasperated when he would support her opinions, cook her a meal, or replace a tire on her bike. What was missing was someone with desires and creativity of his own. "Stop being so nice," she cried. "You're more attractive the other way." Had he launched upon some kind of neurotic head adventure, exploiting everyone around him in a bid for self-dissolution?

One weekend Jane set out with a group of bikers to Dexter, sixteen miles away. Kyle rode far behind, and she regularly slowed down to let him catch up for a drink along the shoulder of road that followed the curve of the Huron River. Halfway there she looked back and didn't see him, She kept going, thinking he had dropped back or stopped to rest. When she cycled into Dexter, he was seated on the village green near the statue of a Civil War soldier. They didn't remember passing each other on the road.

Unnatural things were now happening which he had to accept. Had he fallen into a dream? He read up on empathy, something deeper than sympathy, an intuitive and involuntary sense of what others were feeling, a capacity to know them from the inside, become them. Like what had occurred between him and Ralphy, and Zoot, and now even Jane. Yes, he loved her, but on a lower frequency he knew the attraction had always been rooted in some fancied identification with the unfortunate. How could one lead a normal life without walking over such people, ignoring what one had a moral obligation to feel? Only survival guilt could give these lives any meaning at all.

So slowly Kyle gave way to invisibility. It was an easy letting go. He missed no one because he was everywhere. He was now a witness to everything in life that was not witnessed, which was the whole show. Of course he remained the most kindly of ghosts. In his movements he never allowed himself to pass directly through anyone. He remained a presence in the house to feed his Lab. Jane, who thought he had lit out for California, quickly found someone else, which gave him relief. He felt a void in being unable to directly help people, but that was the price of omnipresence. Only in moments of nostalgia did he miss the feel of sunlight on his skin, wind against his cheek, or a woman's fingers in his tangle of thick blond hair.

Her

I entered the room and the floor lamps left pools of soft light on the carpet that those guests mingling about avoided standing in, choosing rather, or so it seemed, to gather at the margins of light as if contact promised a sudden and perhaps embarrassing disclosure. Perhaps some flash of information that the occasion required be kept secret. But what was this occasion anyway?

An attractive woman was sitting on a couch nearby. Her green eyes floated about and then fastened on me. I could not interpret her level of interest or the nature of her attention, whether or not this was a flirtation. I decided to be optimistic and walked over and sat next to her, careful to leave a proper space between us, a leather cushion actually. She placed a cigarette between her lips, her eyes unblinking, never leaving my face. "Well, give me a light," she said. "Haven't you ever seen this scene before?" Her tone was a blend of contempt and tenderness.

"I don't have a match, don't smoke, but wait a second," I said, rising from the couch. In a nearby leather chair another guest was lifting a lighter beneath his cigarette and I reached out and snatched it from him. He looked at me like this was always happening to him. When I turned back to the couch my place was now occupied by another man, broad-shouldered, wearing a tuxedo and sporting a head of luxurious oiled hair that hung over his temples.

"Excuse me," I said, reaching down to touch his shoulder, "but that seat has been taken, and by me. Please get out of it now."

He ran his hand back through the cascading hair and smiled as if he knew what the future held and that it was good. But he didn't know the future and it wasn't good. Without hesitation I lit the lighter and lowered it near his hair, singeing it, imagining it would burst into a skullcap of flames. The tuxedoed man bolted to his feet and rushed at me, and reflexively I struck him in the face with my fist. He got off the floor and walked away, without direction, although still avoiding the puddles of light cast by the lamps. I followed him and told a waiter standing near the lobby that he was a dangerous arsonist. For some reason the waiter already had a fire extinguisher under his arm, and a moment later squirted white foam into my rival's face and hair, transforming him into a giant snowman in some youth theater production. I reclaimed my place on the couch next to the imperious woman and lit her cigarette. At least I had proven my reliability when assigned a practical task.

"So what's on your mind?" I asked, aware of a seductive odor she gave off in my direction, maybe perfume, maybe a new soap she had used in the shower earlier, when her body was smooth and naked and gleaming with running water. Would I ever see that naked body?

"I've just returned from Florida and my father's funeral," she said. "I was very close to him and need someone to comfort me, even hug me." She looked at me with the same expectancy that she had when she wanted her cigarette lit. So I hugged her and she clung tight, then regained her reserve and continued. "I had flown down all fall to comfort him as he declined, hoping he would die when I was beside him. But I wasn't there when it happened. I was stepping off the plane at the airport when my younger brother informed me that he had left us."

"I'm sorry," I said.

"I didn't really believe he was dead," she whispered confidentially. "At the condo I learned he was at Norwood Funeral Home awaiting cremation. I wanted to see the body one more time, for some reason, although my brother said it was a bad idea, an idea natural enough but one to resist. But I went anyway, driving into a bad section of Riviera Beach. It was so bad that when I parked in the empty lot and went to the door of the funeral home, it was locked. When it cautiously opened, the mortician and his assistant Henry explained they kept the door locked for security. At any time someone might walk in with a gun and spray the place with bullets." She inhaled and pursed her full lips. I couldn't help but notice her left hand was agitated, as if she were squeezing an invisible ball.

"Then why was this funeral home chosen?" I asked.

"I don't know. We are quite affluent. My father had been attending a Catholic church in the neighborhood. He liked the all-black choir even though he spent his whole life among racists. Maybe that was why, some kind of spiritual atonement, though I don't really know. Anyway I was directed to a small chapel just off the lobby. It was empty, just a few rows of pews, except for my father who was laid out on a table up front." She paused. "I approached him slowly until I was standing next to the body. They had dressed him in a dark blue suit, white shirt and blue tie with broad yellow diagonal stripes. The attire was appropriately conservative, except when I looked at my father's face I didn't recognize him. The forehead was too brief and narrow, shorn of muscle tissue, the eye sockets too sunken and close together, the mouth lipless and small, nearly a straight line like a mailbox slot. This was just not my father's body, and for a brief instant I had an insane impulse to run into the lobby and announce there had been a mistake. But it was him, his remains at least. I bent down and kissed him on the forehead, then broke out weeping. He was dead, indeed gone, literally gone: this was a body all right but without the spirit that made it real. I hadn't thought my father was dead because I had never seen him dead and could not imagine it. But here was the proof. It was the only time I emotionally lost it throughout the entire funeral proceedings that weekend. Some poet, I can't remember which one, said that after the first death there is no other."

That night at her apartment, freed from the social gathering and dangerous pools of light, I did get to see and touch her naked body. I wasn't slighted that I was providing her with grief therapy more than passion, I was just thankful for the turn of events that led here. Her talk seemed to be preparing me for a moment in my own future. "My father was a secret romantic," she said, her back to me in the bed, my arm slipped around her waist. "Every spring, on the anniversary of my mother's death, he would drive at dusk up the coast to Jupiter and from the end of a wharf throw a bouquet of flowers into the ocean to seek her ashes. His ashes were handled more unceremoniously. My brother swam out beyond the breakers with the container, but the wind was blowing, and when he cast the ashes they blew back into his face and mouth. Both he and a group of friends and relatives watching from the beach were laughing wildly . . ."

Her story made me think of the man at the party covered with fire extinguisher foam, but that memory passed in a flash, replaced by a vast placid image of the Atlantic ocean quietly filling up with human ashes.

B. J.

He coached the Detroit Jets, the only youth soccer team in Detroit, recruited from the neighborhood. The team was largely black, with a few Irish and Italian kids and his son thrown in. They practiced on an empty patch of grass in Palmer Park, and after checking for dog shit and glass, he set up orange cones and schooled the boys in dribbling, trapping, heading, and short linked passing. Young Chaldeans would drift across Woodward Avenue to join an afternoon scrimmage, or drug addicts wander by for a glassy-eyed look. One afternoon an ambulance and police car pulled up and attendants dragged two bodies out of the nearby woods. On Saturdays they crossed Eight Mile into Ferndale and the northern suburbs for games against all-white teams. They quickly earned respect for their excellent play. He loved the boys, and was especially endeared to B. J. Williams, his diminutive right midfielder, who could propel his compact body down a soccer field like a propeller without a plane.

But race was always the banner that waved when they took the field. In Grosse Pointe, a wealthy suburb northeast of Detroit, they played the Hurricanes. A young girl, maybe sixteen, perhaps a high school player, was referee, and throughout the first half every time a free ball was cleanly contested by a white Hurricane and a black Jet, she blew her whistle. A free kick awarded to the Hurricanes. He saw no physical contact was required, just proximity. The calls grew more absurd, and the Jets more hesitant and dismayed. When two Hurricanes ran into each other and a foul was called on Marcus Borus, standing five yards away, he objected from the sidelines and was yellow-carded.

"Okay," he told the team at half time, "we all have to forget the ref. Just play on."

The girl's apartheid hallucinations continued into the second half. He controlled his emotions, but a few black parents behind him were vocally upset, recognizing what was transpiring. With ten minutes left, standing at midfield, the girl called a penalty kick on a handball clearly five yards outside the Jets' penalty box. Next she walked over to Joel, warning the lanky goalkeeper not to move off his line until after the shot was taken. The Hurricane scuffed the penalty kick, but Joel stood nailed to his line as the ball dribbled into the corner of the goal.

He walked onto the field and was red-carded.

In the parking lot the Grosse Pointe coach, who apologized for the refereeing, consoled him. "I guess you can tell," he said, "what we dream about Detroit." "No damage done." He watched the Jets and the Hurricanes walk off the field on friendly terms, and imagined detecting in the victors a mood of sympathetic thoughtfulness.

When the Jets were under-11s, he arranged a special event. Two matches in Kincardine, Canada, a small Scotch-Irish village on Lake Huron some 180 miles up the coast from Windsor. When he told B. J., the boy flashed his characteristic grin – wide, mischievous, ultimately mysterious. They drove up in two vans, a raucous group that sobered up under the spell of mile after mile of Ontario farmland to the east, the deep blues of Huron to the west. They checked into an old motel abutting a turn in a curling river, horses grazing on the far bank.

The village sat on a bluff above the lake, and one could traverse its picturesque downtown with a couple of good corner kicks. They walked the main street, parents and boys, smiling at people so regularly blue-eyed, ruddy-cheeked, and red-haired it made them blink. The people of Kincardine blinked right back at them.

They played two matches that weekend against the strongest under-14 team in the province of Ontario, on a hard sloping field swept by winds off the lake so strong that any high clearing kick could boomerang back over your head. The Highlanders won both games by lopsided shutouts. Yet they were amazed by the relentless, headlong efforts of the black team from Detroit, and especially B. J. By the second half they were interrupting their attacks to help up smaller Jets they had just sent flying for excessive friskiness.

But the amazement of the Highlanders went deeper. Most had never been in the presence of a black person. An hour after the first loss, the Jets and parents were downtown at the Melvin Tavern, gathered around tables in the back, wolfing down hamburgers and fries. He noticed when a few Highlanders walked in, still in uniform. They drifted to the back, on a mission, moving up behind the team. Suddenly one boy reached out and touched B. J.'s hair. *Kinky hair!* Another Highlander, with a shy smile, did the same. B. J. grinned, then pulling the taller boy closer, reached up to touch his bowl of red hair. Half a dozen citizens of Kincardine looked on from the bar. What happened next didn't surprise him. Tiny and black, B. J. stood up and moved deliberately down the bar, stopping at every stool to extend his right hand in friendship, and glancing away, offer his hair for the touching. Each time his left hand fell over the white hand in a kind of casual blessing.

Sailing

Alesia was twenty-four, and until losing her first-born child to sudden infant death syndrome the previous winter, had known little but happiness and success. A pale beauty with a shock of straw-colored hair, she had won honors as a high school swimmer, was a creative student and popular across a range of rival groups. It surprised no one when she went to Brown on a scholarship, then on to the University of California for graduate study in English. The details surrounding her second year in Berkeley were obscure, but rumors floated back about her involvement with the counter-culture and drugs. The news of her illegitimate child came as a shock to her parents and friends. She was living alone in an apartment off Telegraph Avenue when she awoke that January morning to discover her four-month-old son on his stomach in the battered crib, still beautiful, but faint blue and still.

She dropped out of school, her whereabouts unknown for months, but returned home to Michigan that summer. Avoiding any contact with her parents in the affluent suburbs north of Detroit, she headed north to Charlevoix.

There she sought out her cousin, who she knew was departing on a sailing expedition. After conferring with him all night in a local tavern, she joined up as a member of the crew, handling the sails and ropes. By nightfall of the first day they reached High Island, tiny and uninhabited off the coast of Lake Michigan, and anchored offshore, a lantern hanging midway up the mast. Already she felt a bond with the other crewmembers, though it had nothing to do with their irrepressible sense of adventure, which contrasted with her own transcendental blankness.

The next day they disembarked and hiked across the virgin waist of the island, a distance of eight miles. At various moments along the way she passed through a series of radiant new identities. She was a saint standing in the middle of a hushed meadow with butterflies draped like lace on her ankles. She was a carefree adolescent swinging across a ravine on a thick rope mysteriously hanging from a high inaccessible limb. She was an armed guerilla scrambling her way through thick undergrowth up to an abandoned grass airfield on the central ridge of her occupied native land. Emerging from the rugged terrain far ahead of the others, she reached the high dune cliffs on the west coast of the island, now a conquistador laying claim to a new world. Iridescent green bees busy in the wildflowers around her, she stood transfixed by the infinite blue expanse of lake.

They slept on board that night, and the next morning set sail, moving from shore into heavy overcast and slate-colored waters. By noon they encountered a threat of storm, sailing into vaporous haze and low, steadily amassing clouds. All this only sharpened the edge of her strange premonition. Gradually a soft amber light descended upon the lake. Visibility grew obscure, but still she made out images of a shoreline and signs of a wreck. There were adults and wooden planks floating in the water, voices calling from the shore in a state of lamentation. Yet their corporeality and placement in the geography was uncertain, flickering like a weak visual pulse. As they sailed deeper into this realm, she found herself underwater – being towed from the stern of the sailboat by a long rope. Steadily pulling herself forward, she reached the foot of the slicing keel and hung there, propelled through the water at a clean terrific speed. Her vision of the underwater world was perfect. Then she saw it – another sailing vessel, sunk on the bottom, pinched against the submerged shoreline. Half of it was torn away as if cleaved for dissection. There, lined up in what had been below deck were rows of drowned babies, like kewpie dolls, only quite real, their eyelids and mouths fluttering open and shut, open and shut, as if they were blinking and chattering away with the movement of the current. She swam to the surface with her revelation, frantic to warn those clinging to planks not to sink below. She appealed to her own crew to stay at their posts before she went back under.

The Pinch Hitter

I sat at the far end of the dugout in a litter of paper cups as the game moved into the seventh inning, still scoreless, and our manager made no signs, gave no indications of any kind that I would figure in the game. I was confident I could hit the opposing St. Louis Cardinal pitcher, that mediocre curveball and zippy but straight fastball, that I could cover shortstop and keep some ground balls from skipping through the infield, that I could turn the clutch double play, that I could make the strong relay from shallow left field to cut down an overreaching runner trying to score. I was a little bit of perfection on the bench, a piece of gold, but never recognized as such. Instead, I had been ignored as an unknown player who would never have been called up at the midseason break without the insistence of the owner who had known my father, having taken fishing trips with him into Canada years ago. I looked at the manager watching our batters walk to the plate in the seventh inning, only to return to the bench vexed and irritated when they were retired. I wiped the perspiration from under my cap and studied our manager

– white hair sticking out from under his cap, which hid a major bald spot, eyes a piercing blue, skin leathered and wrinkled and turned a desert red from a long summer in the sun. He projected an image of authority and competence, but the team was losing morale and staggering under that authority. I recognized his reputation had stayed consistently favorable for too long, a bubble created by the media, the triumph of pontifical grandstanding over the obvious truth. Maybe his smoking that left him with offensive breath partially concealed by Doublemint gum biased me; maybe it was his addiction to superstitious impulses. Paul Gibson would pitch on two days' rest because a red warbler kept tapping on his hotel window that morning; George Anderson would switch from center to right field because the outfield grass was mowed very short that night; Larry Evans would pinch-hit in San Francisco because his maroon bat matched the paint bordering the top of the outfield fence. But no one in particular noticed this, except me, and no one was overly concerned about our fall in the standings, which made me more and more eager to make an appearance in the lineup. But our manager never gave me the slightest attention.

My reason for wanting to play this particular afternoon was not clear to me. We had fallen into a losing streak that now stood at a dozen games. We were ending up a home stand with the Cardinals and they broke open the game that day with three runs in the top of the ninth. We rallied impotently in our last at-bats, loading the bases with two outs with the help of an error and two walks. Standing alone on the steps of the dugout, the manager looked down his bench and his eyes fell on Larry Evans, but before he announced his decision, I sprang up and was standing in front of him. His breath withered me and his blue eyes blazed death into my face. "Skipper," I said, "let me pinch-hit. I know I can hit this guy. Rotting away on the bench has prepared me like a putrid tomato to be thrown in the face of the Cardinals. The fans are hungry for a victory and I can give you a lift, get the town off your back, and placate the owner of this team. What do you say?" I was able to talk in this fashion at the most unexpected moments. The manager stared at me like I was an intrepid cockroach, but I continued. "Skipper, I know you haven't bothered to check out my abilities, just as you don't know you have prostate cancer, or that I am sleeping with the owner's daughter, whereas complete self-knowledge is the source of real strength, a cure for the ineffectual. Your willful in-completeness has led to many bad decisions on the field, in particular the waste of one of your most talented play-ers. I'm speaking of myself. Frankly, I foresee you with-out a job next spring unless you turn things around. The owner's daughter told me that much. You can tell from my mind at work that I can turn things around. What do you say?" The umpire was standing on the lip of the dugout reminding the manager that the Pirates needed a batter at the plate and right now. With a look of nausea, he cocked his eyebrow at me and nodded toward the field.

A charge of energy and fear went through me as I turned to the rack and pulled out a black lacquered bat. As I walked to the plate, the loudspeaker mispronounced my name as if it were a word from some foreign language. It was a scuffed-up mess of chalk around home plate, but the smell of dirt rose sweet and strong in my nostrils. "Play ball!" It was the plate umpire signaling me into the batter's box. I dug my cleats in and smoothly pointed the bat toward the pitcher – a tall angular kid, maybe six-four, looking cocky, maybe because he was facing an unknown player with the game on the line. The height of the mound made it seem like he was standing on a ladder and about to touch the sky. His frame was pinched between the breasts of a young Hooter's waitress painted on a huge billboard above the centerfield bleachers. On either side you could see the sooty office buildings of downtown Pittsburgh. I felt relaxed, confident. My teammates on the bases took their leads, yelling encouragement like we were all close friends with their hopes riding on me and their expectations high. The first pitch was an overpowering fastball on the inside corner, not a chance of hitting it, and my bat stayed frozen in position. "Strike one!" I stepped out of the batter's box and clunked some dirt caught in my spikes, then looked down to the third-base coach, who ignored me. Instead he picked up a rosin bag and stashed it in his pocket as if he were gathering equipment to take off the field. I was unperturbed, just stepped back into the box, took a sinker that came in like a waist-high fast-ball, then dropped just as it reached me to my kneecaps. "Strike two!" The manager glared at me from the dugout like I was some leper crashing a health spa. I stared abstractly over the shortstop's head and settled into the box again. The next pitch was an outside waste pitch and I swung and just ticked it, fouling it off.

Then something happened, quite without intention, an amazing sequence of twenty pitches, all of which I fouled off – a curve ball into the dirt, two fastballs against the screen, a slider down the third-base line, a fast ball into the catcher's mitt and out, my contact gradually improving, two sharp grounders outside both foul lines, a pop-up into the stands behind third base, a soft Chinese liner behind third again, a foul fly into the right field boxes, a liner outside the third base line, a fly deep to left that cleared the fence ten feet to the left of the foul pole. The pattern, still emerging, was catching some attention. Even the most distracted fans in the stands, the bored girlfriends, the truant teenagers, the simple drunks, the Iraq veterans in wheelchairs in the upper deck, all recognized that I was at least a capable hitter who just might come through and win the game. That is, once these preliminary foul balls subsided. I was in the same zone I had been all game, even on the bench, but the pitches flung toward me were coming in big as grapefruits, the ball sharper, its stitched seams bright red, the spin a dead giveaway for whether the pitch was a fastball, curve, change, sinker, slider. I even lined a knuckle ball into the Cardinal dugout. As the foul balls continued, the crowd grew more drawn in, differently focused, irresistibly galvanized, for how could this sequence be happening?

By now, I had struck maybe forty foul balls into the stands and the gangly pitcher was bent over, seemed to sway on the mound like a wind-blown sapling. I just kept fouling off pitches, gradually enjoying the buildup and release of tension with each pitch and swing, gradually forgetting the game situation altogether, gradually changing my goal, desiring only to keeping this going. And the fans did as well, cheering louder and louder as my exploration of protracted non-achievement continued. Was my performance some kind of involuntary but symbolic protest against the game itself, its pollution by steroid use, its absurd salaries, its neglect of me? I sensed now that the fans might be disappointed if I drove in the winning runs and ended the game.

"Jesus Christ!" the plate umpire gasped, stopping the game to receive a new stash of baseballs. The Cardinal manager removed the lanky kid from the mound and replaced him with a veteran reliever with a rubber arm. At one point I broke my bat on an inside fastball and when I returned to the dugout to get another one, the manager said, "Are you doing this on purpose, to extend an at-bat you'll never get again?" "Maybe," I said, "or maybe I'm just getting a bead on these pitchers. Then again I may be creating a pinch game that is still up for grabs." Picking a new bat, I noticed that my hands were red and swollen, some blood seeping from under my fingernails. But I returned to the batter's box and the pattern continued: a bouncer to our third-base coach, a foul deep to right, and a foul ball after a checked swing. I noticed the Cardinal infielders were standing around now like they were waiting at a bus stop, indifferent, probably getting hungry for dinner. I had been at the plate for almost an hour and the sun, a smudgy gold disc, was sinking behind the Hooter's billboard. The crowd's reaction too was evolving from excited disbelief to mute expectancy, then to unmistakable signs of boredom. Fans were starting to leave the ballpark. My predictability at the plate had left the inherent drama of the ninth inning far behind. The novelty of what I was doing was gradually being reinterpreted as lack of competence, delay, a lack of any will to win the game. Now, with each foul ball, I heard murmurs of discontent, some booing from the bleachers. I was becoming a symbol of tedium and indecision, of their lives and my own, exactly what they had come to the ballpark to escape. If I were sitting among them I would go unnoticed, but on the diamond at home plate I was holding up a mirror to them and dressed in a baseball uniform no less.

I was a genius at self-derogatory analysis and here was another example, another opportunity. I had to put an end to this inexplicable anomaly l was dramatizing, but didn't know whether to climax it with a game-winning home run or a strikeout. I stepped out of the batter's box for a rest, as well I might, my fingernails smeared with blood, but mainly to think about what the crowd, what was left of it, wanted to see as finale to my appearance as a pinch hitter. They had all but forgotten about the outcome of the game; it was more like they were witnessing some freak on the street corner who had nothing to do with baseball, or who had invented a new game that they had grasped and were intrigued with long enough to put baseball out of mind, only to abandon interest in something so exceptionally meaningless. What conclusion to my performance would be most gratifying for them? What was in it for them? What fantasy was my pinch-hitting fulfilling, or maybe destroying?

"Play ball!" the umpire growled and I stepped back into the box. The next pitch was fat, right down the pipe with no speed or curve on it, batting-practice stuff, and I almost swung and missed, just a tip that popped out of the catcher's mitt. Then another fat pitch, and another that I continued to stroke hard but still foul. Then it dawned on me that the new Cardinal reliever was grooving them on purpose, wanted me to clear the bases and end this weirdness, even if it meant losing the game. I was stunned because the whole purpose of the game, winning, I had subverted, and oddly enough if I performed at this instant like I wanted to when I first walked to the plate, I might not be cheered but booed. The human crowd was that stupid, fickle, irrational. Then I swung at the last pitch and caught it perfectly on the fat part of the barrel and the ball shot out toward the left field fence and silence fell upon the ballpark. Eyes watched the ball ricochet into the empty seats to the left of the Hooter's billboard. I dropped the bat and circled the bases, the silence broken by a few boos that sounded like cows in a far pasture. The Cardinal infielders stared at me like I was a hot dog vender who had leapt onto the field and was mischievously trotting around the bases. Fans stood up, turned their backs, and moved toward the exits. When I crossed home plate there, there were no teammates to greet me, even the umpires had disappeared, and when I approached the dugout, the bench was empty and cleared of equipment. It was as if what I had done showed a lack of respect, represented a dishonoring of the game, not the home run but the length of time hitting foul ball after foul ball at the plate until the very meaning of the game of baseball had been placed in limbo and then dismissed.

I repeat none of this was by intention. It was impossible to deliberately do what I had done, foul off almost one hundred pitches, probably more, and yet it seemed somehow symbolic of my career and contribution to baseball. I was a subversive and utterly insignificant. I strolled out to short centerfield and felt cleansed, uplifted by the arriving dusk. The memory of the day was fading and pigeons flew up under the lid of the upper deck, retiring for the day. The outfield grass was thick and pungent, somehow as virgin as a freshly discovered mountain valley. Walking back to the dugout, I passed by a groundskeeper I knew and he never looked up from his rake. In the locker room, I was not congratulated or even recognized by my teammates, but the collective rejection was much deeper than the indifference I had faced all season. It was like I had committed some incalculable offense. The manager called me into his office and announced I was being released immediately and to clear out my belongings. I shrugged and didn't say a word since he had demonstrated to me all season that he had no intelligence or judgment. The treatment from the players did hurt, but what had happened this afternoon was so irrational, so mysterious that a response to it could be equally so. I didn't shower, left my uniform on the floor, and walked out into the streets of Pittsburgh filled with pedestrians and honking cars and the faint promise of early evening in urban America.

The Party

He threw a party and all the friends of his twenties miraculously appeared. They had been scattered all over the country, yet here they were. There were Dartmouth classmates he had not seen in two decades, one now head of the World Monetary Fund, another running an environmental nonprofit in D.C. There was Anna, a girlfriend of his in Pittsburgh, now living on a kibbutz in Israel. Alex had appeared, now a veterinarian in Boulder, and Amy, who taught elementary school in inter-city Detroit. And there was Mark, a free spirit who after graduating from Dartmouth had gone straight into the bush of Vietnam, serving two years as a "squid" or medic with the Marines. The evening was as successful as he could have dreamed, reminding him of parties years ago when they were young and this was all happening for the first time. Losing himself in talk, drinking, and dancing with true friends, those of his own generation who can never be replaced, he forgot that he was hosting the party for others, important fundraisers he had never met, at the request of IBM, his current employer. But none of those people had arrived. Only his friends had appeared from the banishment of adulthood.

At the end of a long evening, when everyone was preparing to leave, the actual guests of the party walked in the front door. He was standing next to Mark with a glass of bourbon in his hand. They were well dressed, formidable in bearing, and wearing insolent smiles. There was some awkwardness due to their inexplicable air of proprietorship. Then with suave deportment they pulled out black Lugers and announced, as if for late night entertainment, that he and his friends were to be executed. There was bustle and terror. Friendship was no defense now. Some were ordered into the large dining room, while others, including Anna, were bound and led into back bedrooms.

He made eye contact with Mark, who had to be experiencing some kind of flashback. Simultaneously they made a break from the house. An opportune moment, the climb through an open window, and the two were running across damp glistening grass. Gunshots popped in the night like firecrackers. They separated among the suburban houses, but instinctively reconnoitered. He did not know where Mark had found the array of weapons, but now they were armed themselves. His house, dimly lit, loomed across the street. They spoke with lucid gravity of rescuing the others.

"Listen," Mark said, his voice soft but clipped, "there are five of them. Circle around to the back of the house and I'll be on the front lawn. I'll take out as many as I can from there. The sniper scope will find them at the windows. When you hear an explosion, a grenade going off, move in through the back door while I keep them occupied. Be steady and shoot to kill, the head or high in the chest. Keep firing. Don't hesitate if they use someone as a shield." Mark paused to stare at him. "This is endgame. Aim for what's exposed and ice them. Understand?"

Blood pounded in his temples. He stared at the Luger and clutched it tightly. He'd never known real combat, yet was eager, fearless. He never felt more alive.

Out-of-Work Line

For Len it was another stint down at the Detroit branch of the Michigan Employment Security Commission. It didn't matter when you arrived. The line began a step inside the windowless steel doors of a squat one-floor building and weaved snake-like from sidewall to sidewall. A security guard kept the line in shape, weeding out stray drunks and other casualties of the recession, shepherding newcomers with stricken faces to the rear.

Today Len gave the guard a nod of recognition. This was his 54th week of collecting unemployment benefits and surely he'd earned that right. New applicants sat in folding chairs off to the right, awaiting interviews, chin on chest, like bundles dropped from the ceiling. Now and then, a defeated temper tantrum would signal a lost form. Those in line just smiled knowingly and yawned.

The line inched forward like a parade of dominoes. Len was a carpenter but also a member of Mensa, and recognized the golden rule that preserved order. No one who arrived later than another person ever left earlier. With that elemental fairness came a remarkable tolerance of delay. The minute hand on the wall clock would leap abruptly ahead, sucking everyone into a backwash of lost connections. By now Len's losses included his wife and social circle, as well as colleagues at construction sites, but others here had lost much more. Health, identity, will to live. Most just stared at the floor or ceiling as if reading some messianic script. Some talked quietly. Paperbacks and newspapers bloomed. Others just checked each other out, taking a fresh look with each weave of the line.

Two weeks ago a man just ahead of Len, upon reaching the counter to collect his check, turned with a glance at his watch and announced, "One hour on the dot."

"That's not bad."

"No, sir," the man said with an ambivalent grin. "Not a bad hourly wage at all."

The trouble was everyone in line worked only one hour every two weeks.

The line showed no sign of malnutrition yet. *Those* people were caught in the crevices of the city, in neighborhoods and states of mind beyond the reach of unemployment checks. Len had flirted with meth for a few months, but was still part of the mainstream. Ahead of him was an elderly couple, behind him two brawny men who'd been pumping a lot of iron. The line was as a democratic blend of chemists, secretaries, manual laborers, autoworkers, businessmen, teachers – you name it. They were united by a common bond of bad luck and stoicism.

Len had the feeling a lot of talent and character was going wasted in this line.

Beyond the far counter was an acre of metal desks, a zone where spirit slumbered as employees of the state of Michigan processed claims under sallow ceiling lights. Their skin was blanched from reviewing so many forms, and at times they seemed paralyzed with their noses in manila folders.

The crush of numbers over recent months had expedited matters at the counter. "Have you had any income this week?" "No." Always the same question, the same reply. Len had repaired some neighborhood porches – undeclared work for small change – as had many in the line. Yet they met with no suspicion these days and passed through like clumps of snow falling off a roof.

Conversation in the line veered toward the basic: the weather, the Tigers, abrupt firings, the job hunt. "I packed the family in the van and went to Texas," a man told Len. "Nothing down there. Texans ain't so friendly either. They tailgate Michigan license plates, drive you right off the road. We came home."

He overheard little talk of politics in the line. People seemed reluctant to link their joblessness to policies out of Washington. But times were changing. Last month, a black man with a chortling bass voice and walrus mustache turned to Len and observed, "That Reagan ain't worth two dead flies."

It was the scientific precision of that *two* that thrilled him and cinched the case.

People continued to bounce on the trampoline as life went on, heading nowhere. Indeed, for Len the highlight of the line was the kids. Young mothers had their hands full. An hour's wait in a crowded, stuffy public space could tax a kid's patience. By afternoon, the wake of crumbs and puddled milk made the footing hazardous.

Last spring his eighteen-month-old son had waited with him for two hours, then finally broke loose. He cut through the line like a shark through a school of blues and, to accompanying cheers, was out the door. Len sprinted after him, and bribed him back with a last remaining cracker.

But for Len, standing in line all these months had been largely meditation. He had time to think about receiving "benefits" for losing his job. He hadn't objected. It enabled him to survive, although not to find a job since there weren't any. It felt a little like getting something for nothing, but the guilt was not crushing. It cast the "system" in a benevolent light, taking the edge off his desperation for now. It seemed to dull political rebellion, making everyone a little soft, lethargic, passive. It acted like a painkiller – enclosing them in a rubber bumper as they floated through the days.

No sharp economic edges, not yet.

In this sense, unemployment benefits set Len and his

mates up for a nasty fall. He had one more check coming. Then nothing. Having passed through the "system," he would no longer be counted among the unemployed, lose even his status as a negative statistic. All of them stood here in the line, in decent spirits, feeling a quiet solidarity – until their time ran out and they fell into an economic black hole.

Then the struggle began for keeps.

Underdog

I entered as a middleweight in the novice division of the
Detroit Golden Gloves. I was forty-eight and had never
boxed before. The tournament was held in an old wood-
en field house in a far corner of the State Fairgrounds on
Woodward Avenue. I hadn't deliberated much on the decision because that wasn't necessary. My whole life was
behind it. Nobody running the tournament had noticed
my age on the application, and probably didn't care.

That Thursday night I parked my car in a grassy lot and
walked into the field house. I could glimpse in the distance, under high rafters, a boxing ring in the middle of
a huge dirt oval designed for horse shows. I edged along
the wall until I came upon the door to a tiny locker room.
Inside were unpainted cinderblock walls, and there I met
the corner man assigned to me. Jerome was black, with
a shaved head, and tender red eyes that seemed to have
looked upon everything life had to offer. His body was
huge and hard as a bowling ball. Half apologizing, I told
him I had found nobody to act as my second, except maybe
some enemies. "No problem, man," he grunted. "I gotcha

covered." He handed me some pale blue boxing trunks with dark stains on the front that I guessed was blood. "Put these on," he ordered. Then he proceeded to wrap my fists with white tape that smelled like fragrant flowers. He paused when he saw a thin red line climbing up the inside of my leg. "You had heart by-pass?" I nodded. "Tell me now," he said, his curiosity mixed with vexation. "Jus' what the fuck you doin' in the Gloves?"

I held my hands out and waited for him to pull on the gloves, which he did, pushing me backwards. Then I started to shadowbox, throwing punches toward the pea-green lockers that smelled of old sweat. "You ever box before?" There was no need to answer that. The punches I was throwing in the air said it all – provisional, exploring some new motion with my arms, like a toddler learning to walk.

"But I have watched boxing all my life," I told Jerome, continuing to shadowbox. "You know, bobbing and weaving in front of a TV screen. Always rooting for the underdog. The trouble is, I've never been in the ring, never been hit, and so this identification with the underdog seems suspect. Vicarious, or voyeuristic, or laced with survivor guilt, something like that."

Jerome wiped his mouth, and gave a resigned shake of his head. "Man, I heard it all now." A roar reached us through the partially opened locker room door. "Well, buddy," he said, "let me tell you somethin'. Our strategy goin' out there is to survive, but I promise you this. You gonna get yur wish. You gonna get hit."

It sounded like a prediction I could count on. A current of fear passed quickly through me. Actually I had endured plenty of blows in my life. Fighting for respect on half a dozen playgrounds when growing up in various states. Concussions playing high school football and college soccer. Muggings in Detroit at gunpoint, one with my eighteen-month-old son standing beside me. But those experiences had been a mixture of accident and bad luck, the turns of fortune that can happen to anyone. The Golden Gloves was different, a choice, pure volition. Now I was recasting myself as the classic underdog, stepping right into the line of fire, displaying that allegiance to victims that had haunted me my whole life.

Leaving the locker room, Jerome and I brushed by a young boxer heading back in. Below his left eye was a huge purple welt, like some animal had burrowed under the skin. Dust rose from the dirt floor of the field house as we walked down an aisle between folding chairs. The ring was elevated and flooded with light, standing out in the murky air like a reef. I climbed up splintered wooden steps and stepped inside the ropes. My leather headgear hid my age from the sparse, almost entirely black crowd. My body was lean and muscled, pale, almost delicate. Without contacts, my vision was blurred. That and the overhead lights blinded me to concrete details except for a frail white octogenarian leaning on the ring apron, prepared to count for the knockdowns with a tiny wooden mallet.

My Croatian last name, Stansa, was mispronounced over the microphone when the bout was announced. I was signaled to the center of the ring by the referee, a broad-chested Hispanic man with thick eyebrows and pockmarked cheeks. On his other side stood my opponent, a gleaming black hydrant named Buddy Alpert, who returned my neutral gaze with a baleful vacancy. His grin seemed to express both cockiness and disbelief. Tugging down my high-riding trunks, the referee noticed a bandage on my abdomen covering the insertion site of my insulin pump. He recognized what he saw, because his face turned into blinking brown stone.

"Keep yur hands up," Jerome ordered as the bell sounded for the first round. I shuffled out from my corner. So this was where I wanted to be, inside the ring, with some dues to pay. The next two minutes had the abysmal disorientation of a hypoglycemic episode, the kind that had landed me in the ER at Henry Ford Hospital many times. My hands up, I bobbed and weaved as if back in front of a TV screen, but Buddy Albert's fists were real. They smashed through my barrier of forearms and elbows. I felt sudden pain, then no pain, just white stars like in cartoons, distant shock, the punches raining down, and then blood filling my mouth. I couldn't escape Albert. Too strong, young, and aggressive. It didn't occur to me to throw a single punch. At one moment I lay on the canvas staring at the octogenarian, listening to his mallet pounding the apron. But when the bell sounded, I was standing up.

"Listen to me!" Jerome shouted in the corner, wiping away blood from my nose. "You can take it, buddy, but you gotta deliver some hurt too. Otherwise I'm stoppin' this thing!"

I heard him and rose from the stool. My gloves felt like small boulders, but I raised them up again. I knew I was falling short even as an underdog. Wasn't what I admired most about them was that they fought back whatever the odds? The ring came alive again with light, crowd noise, and incipient mayhem. Maybe enough was enough. From some unknown source I felt a new dispensation, something that had been missing all my life: permission to kill or be killed. At the bell I moved out unsteadily toward Buddy Albert.

Mitch and Georgia

Mitch was a handsome yellow Lab who had died of cancer two years past and went directly to heaven. He enjoyed himself there, despite the fact that it wasn't a very doggy place. No trees or hydrants to pee on, rotten stuff to roll around in, TV remotes to chew on, bedroom slippers to drop in the toilet. All favorite things he did when he was alive. God did not take him on walks in the woods or swimming in lakes because Heaven was just an endless expanse of fluffy white clouds.

Not that He would have bothered. God was known to be angry and vengeful, as Mitch was aware, having chewed on a Bible long enough to know that the deity had ordered the killing of a million unbelievers in the Old Testament alone, usually through the razing of cities, rape and slaughter. And being a water rescue dog, he remembered the forgotten 20 million who couldn't find room on board Noah's ark during the Flood. Mitch, on the other hand, was always forgiving, always, happier to see Mathew the later his owner stepped through the front door. God just sat on His throne all day, calmly dreaming up new catastrophes He knew would create new Christian converts on earth, since people needed hope and would swallow anything to find it.

So what did Mitch enjoy about heaven anyway? It turned out that through a gap in the fluffy clouds he had a good view of the back yard where he grew up. He could often see Mathew down there mowing the grass, and recently with an unfamiliar, lovely dog running around. One day God climbed off his throne to peer down too, and told Mitch that her name was Georgia, and warned him not to have any sinful thoughts about her, since thoughts were deeds, and bad deeds were as forbidden in heaven as they were on earth. A common dog better watch out because He was omniscient. Mitch didn't know what that word meant, so his surveillance of the chocolate Lab from high above went on until he fell totally in love.

To be lovelorn in heaven is not a happy prospect. Mitch was now desperate to get out of a place that couldn't even offer squirrels in trees much less female dogs. But the angels, without gender, fluttering about like half-visible gossamers, were useless. Paradoxically there was nobody to help him but God. Mitch tried to summon up some leap of faith, but it was hard to leap in clouds. Now battling sinful thoughts, he started hanging out around His throne, seeking favor, careful not to absent-mindedly lift up a hind leg. As with people, he could read God's thoughts before they came to Him. And here was a vain and lonely deity, and knowing everything, probably bored to death. So Mitch took a chance. He told God that he ought to be sent back to earth as His messenger. Not another Jesus, heavens no, but just a creature to spread the Word. Mitch showed Him how he could stand up on his hind legs like a preacher and yap. Something flashed in God's head. The following morning Mitch found himself in his back yard as if he had never left. Waiting for life to stir inside the house, he couldn't help comparing himself to Jesus, just a little bit, but more rebellious.

Suddenly Georgia pushed through the flap of the dog door, her radiant brown fur gleaming in the morning light. She looked at Mitch and blinked. His panting heart ignited a memory, and racing straight to the back fence, he disappeared into the overgrowth in a frenzy of digging, and reappeared with a huge, earth-blackened bone in his jaws. He trotted back to George and dropped the bone at her feet. It was a serious offering, something he had gnawed on long before she ever arrived. She eyed the bone for a minute, then delicately took it in her jaws and went back inside through the dog door. Blinded by love, Mitch interpreted this as reciprocity of feeling, that she loved him and not the bone, and so followed her through the dog door. He was inside the house he had dreamed about every night in heaven.

"Mitch! You're back!"

Mathew raced from the living room and threw his arms

around his beloved dog, mysteriously home at last. Mitch inhaled his human scent, felt those fingers scratch behind his ears in just the right places, oh yes, how he loved Mathew . . . but where did Georgia go? It was a truly blissful day. Time was unreal. There was no death. Now Mitch's only challenge was to keep Georgia from avoiding him.

It was a rocky road, this courtship. While Georgia had high standards, Mitch was just a dog. He would indifferently pass gas one moment – act morally superior like he had just dropped in from heaven the next. At times he would rise up on hind legs and a gargling noise would issue from his throat. When Mathew took them to the woods, he was insanely jealous when a passing dog would sniff Georgia's behind, and went berserk when she returned the favor. But he persisted because there was nothing else. This was true love. He brought Georgia any animal he caught – mice, squirrels, chipmunks, and dead varmints of every kind. If another dog growled at her in the woods, he would chase the terrified mutt right into the parking lot of the nearby Lutheran church. When Georgia was rushed to the animal hospital to have a corncob removed from her intestine, one he had given her, Mitch lay on her cushion at home for a week, hardly moving except to do his business, passing through the dog door with such slouching despondency one would have thought *his* life was in danger.

And so it was.

When Georgia recovered, she finally began to

acknowledge Mitch's attentions. On winter nights, when it was freezing outside and chilly in the house, she let him press his body against hers as they slept on the comforter covering Mathew in bed. Like a sandbag, she would protect him from any incoming dreams of heaven. When she unburied one of her bones in the back yard and dropped it at Mitch's feet, he looked at her and blinked. When Mathew removed a sliver of glass from his paw and he limped around whimpering for a day, Georgia came up and gently licked it better. Soon they were walking side by side on leash around the block and pairing up while conducting their off-leash investigations in the woods. They became co-conspirators around the house, into petty acts of mischief – plundering the bag of kibble in the closet, swiping meat left on the kitchen counter, dragging piles of clean laundry down the stairs. Anything that was lost in the house could be found lying outside the dog door. The two of them chewed up the manuscript of Mathew's novel, scattering scraps of white Xerox paper around the back yard like confetti.

And so Mitch and Georgia grew happily old together. Sometimes, basking in the sun on the front porch, he would look up at her, napping on the cushioned recliner, and marvel at her beauty. His thoughts now reflected the level of maturity he had reached as a dog. Atheistic thoughts gave way to wondering why Mathew, if he loved him so much, had his nuts cut off, especially when he could use them now. But every time Mitch asked himself that question, Georgia blinked at him, yawned, and went back to sleep. Still, life had been wonderful once he vacated the high fluffy clouds. He had found a better heaven, one without any God on a throne, right on the front porch.

Even if the squirrel, chattering at him upside down from the overarching branch of a chestnut tree, would not shut up.

Mark Steinmetz

Mr. Gullick

There are some memories that do not fade, like initials carved in a tree trunk.

Mr. Gullick was a barely functioning alcoholic who owned Ship Ahoy, a beach club on the Jersey shore, along with a seedy motel on the other side of Route 101. The club was built on a huge wooden platform on stilts above the beach, with rows of lockers looking across a hundred yards of sand to the Atlantic. From twelve to fifteen I worked as a locker boy there with a dozen other kids. We swept out lockers and helped with the daily operation of the club – parking cars, running errands, cleaning up messes, carrying huge sun umbrellas down to the ocean for club members. Every other week Mr. Gullick would leave for electro-shock treatments in NYC. We were young, knew nothing about life, and as locker boys took a certain pride in being linked to this unknown figure, almost thrilled in knowing our boss was drunk much of the day in the motel.

For some reason I became his favorite.

He was a handsome man, in his fifties, fine-featured, his skin creased like a wallet and hair turning gray. He made me think of British colonial officers I had come across reading Rudyard Kipling's *Kim*. Every morning, before the club opened at 7:30, it was my job to deliver fresh coffee to his office. I would stand inside the door and watch him drink, coffee flying from the cup onto the table and floorboards. He was always suffering from the shakes. After he was done the two of us set out for the jetty to the north of the club, Mr. Gullick leading the way, wearing a battered white admiral's hat with a black brim. I trailed along behind, balancing his .22-caliber rifle on my shoulder. We stopped at the surf's edge. The jetty was made up of jet-black boulders piled thirty feet high, maybe sixty feet across, and reached a quarter mile into the Atlantic. We locker boys would scamper out on the jetty during breaks and halfway to the end would dive into the ocean from high boulders. It required guts and good timing to catch the swell of a wave and maximize the ocean's depth to prevent wrecking our bodies on the sand bottom.

But the walk out there had a more serious purpose. This was a hunting expedition – for huge black rats, ten to fifteen pounds, that lived in perfect camouflage on the jetty. Standing knee-deep in the surf, bracing himself against a boulder, Mr. Gullick would ask for his rifle and the two of us, with great vigilance, waited for the rats to appear. It was like watching a fragment of boulder sneaking away. Instantly I shouted, "There!" and my boss opened fire. Sometimes he started shooting without my prompting, pumping bullets into the jetty without aim or reason, hallucinating rats everywhere. "Nick, did you see that one? I blew his head off!" At these moments I was face to face with madness, the whole jetty now the glistening back of a giant rat with nose pointed into the Atlantic. The rifle shots became innocuous pops in the immensity of sky and ocean. When the ammunition was spent, Mr. Gullick handed me the rifle, then marched us back to Ship Ahoy, his head held high, very cinematic, as if embodying the last hope of mankind against some vague free-floating threat.

He deputized me to carry out other assignments that offered a further look into the insanity of things. Ship Ahoy was located in Sea Bright, an hour by train or car from NYC, and the beach club was among the first you reached that was free enough from pollution to allow swimming. On weekends, we drew plenty of refugees from the city and braced for a lot of weird guests. Most Ship Ahoy members were respectable and middle-class, and clashes of life style were bound to occur. Mr. Gullick gave to me the responsibility of handling them. He saw me protecting the values of the Porter family, whose umbrella I lugged from the club down to the ocean every day, their toddler Abbey in my other arm, drooling barf down my bare chest. The rats from NYC might be a threat to them.

"Nick," he informed me one Sunday, "a city couple is screwing down there under that red umbrella. Go break it up, and give them our rates at the motel across the street.

Tell them they have no choice in the matter." By the time I trudged down through hot sand to the red umbrella, now tipped on its side to form a little dugout, club members had already pulled back in shock, creating a little more privacy for the couple. When I peered under the umbrella, they were definitely going at it. The man's pale hairy back to me, knit swim trunks at his ankles, his butt ramming into a pale blonde woman, pieces of her bikini discarded in the sand, legs wrapped loosely around his waist.

"Excuse me," I said, picking a peeling nose, "but the owner of this beach club offers you a cut rate at the motel across the street."

The man turned around, the woman's face hidden by his shoulder. "What's the problem, kid? You can't service your woman out here?"

"The owner sets the rules. No sex on the beach. I just work here."

"Well, your boss is fighting human nature. He must be crazy." I stood there, not contradicting him. "Okay, kid, I won't get you in trouble. So where's the owner? I want to subtract what we paid to get kicked off this beach from the motel rate."

I gave him directions to the office as he pulled up his trunks and she put her bikini back on. I admired how they weaved their way through the checkerboard of family blankets, without embarrassment, just calmly aligned with life's great commandment: reproduce. Mr. Gullick was in no physical or mental condition to advocate that.

Thinking back, he probably saw me as a replacement for his son who died when his Air Force training jet crashed into a mountainside outside Colorado Springs. It was a loss he often brought up in slurred conversation, revisiting his son's feats on the gridiron in high school, his perfect left-handed batting stoke on the diamond. That might have explained his paramilitary possession of me, the policing missions he sent me on, his pleasure in my automatic, unreflecting obedience, and especially his paternal indulgence of both me and the other locker boys whose mischief may have served him as some fanciful reimagining of what must have been a tough boyhood. Actually the locker boys all but destroyed Ship Ahoy beach club. We attacked each other's cleaned lockers with wet sand and stray garbage. From a hole in the attic floor over the women's bathroom we became peeping Toms with promising hard-ons until one day a young member, gazing upward, detected eyes in the ceiling. We parked members' cars in the front lot, lounging all afternoon in the front seats, listening to Yankee or Dodger games on the radio until the batteries behind those huge dashboards went dead.

Through it all we were never fired. Mr. Gullick identified with us. At high tide we swam out to the wooden poles in the ocean marking the swimming area, dove to the bottom with lance guns, shot spider crabs through the shell and pulled them and other trash to shore, clearing out the area for swimmers. He took great pride in the Jersey hurricane season when only lifeguards and locker boys were permitted in the ocean. We put on a daring show, bodysurfing the swelling power of waves twenty feet and higher, crashing and bouncing like corks in the bubbling white surf. Mr. Gullick could have gotten in trouble for allowing this, but the spectacle, watched by hundreds of Ship Ahoy members gathered along the beachfront, proved to him only the immortality of youth.

His own bid for immortality failed the following spring. I was waiting to catch a bus home from baseball practice at Fair Haven High when a headline at the local newsstand caught my eye. *Ship Ahoy Owner Found Dead.* I bought the newspaper and read that Mr. Gullick had killed himself at the deserted beach club while preparing to open for the season. He was found in his office, and there was mention of a .22-caliber rifle at the scene. I was shaken. He was my friend and now he was gone. I knew nothing about his mental turmoil that underlay everything. Staring sightless out the bus window, I wondered what his last thoughts were, whether a morning cup of coffee might have saved him. At the instant of leaving this world did he believe he was shooting the largest rat on the jetty, the one that was always getting away? The thought made me shudder, because it would have been so wrong.

Meat Squad

It was late at night, yet therapeutic to linger a while on the sofa, loosen the prosthesis attached to his right leg at the knee, and go back twenty-odd years to those first two seasons of football at Rumson High. How his gut would fill up with anxiety as last period ticked down in study hall. Whether there was rain or fall sunlight at the tall windows, he felt the lassitude of someone who would soon be ordered to walk in formation across open terrain toward woods alive with the crack of rifle fire. Every afternoon, he watched two rows below him their starting senior guard, a muscular pockmarked gnome named Earl Scholl, hold a cigarette lighter to the seat in front of him and char the wood with fierce concentration. He was just getting ready for practice. Up front the faculty proctor was too preoccupied trying to spot who was arcing pennies high into the air to notice Earl's work. When the pennies came down with a metallic clank across the auditorium, like toy grenades, a ripple of laughter would go up. Anything seemed possible, indeed permissible. When the final bell rang, while students flooded out noisy corridors into airy freedom, he would file down to the locker room.

It was the late fifties, and high school locker rooms were cramped, filled with a gray din, like a holding cell in some county jail. Everything stank. Shoulder pads were always caked with mud or soaked with sweat, rank and stiffening. He was fourteen with acne all over his face, shoulders, back and chest, and pulling on that equipment was like feeding a fire. He remembered once sitting on the bench in front of his locker and popping a huge inflamed pimple on his breastbone. He kept pressing the skin around it until there was a stream of yellow pus running down to his stomach, pooling at the hip, then running down the inside of his thigh until it reached his knee. When he wiped away the pus there was a wound in his pale, thin chest that looked like a bullet hole.

Locker rooms were a logical command post for preparing American boys at the height of the Cold War to be fed into the meat grinder of an inevitable war with Soviet Russia. That was his destiny, and despite the chorus of curses and jokes, slamming metal doors, the mood was somber among the meat squad. At last players would file out into the slant light of afternoon, and cleats clicking on the asphalt, walk across a parking area to the football field. The distant goalposts stuck into the sky like lances. There the team loitered on a grassy knoll to await the arrival of Coach Rosotti. The meat squad sat apart, like orphans, fourteen and fifteen, totally outsized, wearing worn-out equipment, yellow tank tops, unnumbered jerseys, carrying helmets of various colors, their heads poking out of giant shoulder pads like wary turtles. He remembered how the woods beyond the field stood silent and remote, autumn leaves a lovely quilt of red and yellow, almost mystical, having nothing to do with football.

More memories of the meat squad kept drifting into his mind, carrying along a quick, unexpected anxiety. He had a right leg back then, blown off at the knee after stepping on a mine in Vietnam. He struggled up on his good leg to pour himself a glass of bourbon, then hopped back to the sofa.

When practice started, the team operated as a unit, stretching, doing jumping jacks, running laps, occupied with various formational drills. It was like a wholesome boot camp. But soon the drills became violent. Facemasks on helmets were still a couple of years away, and he dreaded in particular the tackling drill. Two dummies were set up about four yards apart, and players formed two lines, facing each other on either side of the opening. At the sound of the whistle, a player at the head of one line ran with the football between the dummies. The player at the head of the other did a somersault and met the charging runner in the opening. He remembered one afternoon he came out of his somersault late and rose up to catch a knee square in the face. He got up groggy and went to the back of the other line, where Mr. Early, the high school principal, who had stopped by to watch practice, started talking to him long enough to recognize that though standing up, he was out cold. He was led away with a cracked cheekbone and concussion, and the next two days became a permanent hole in his memory. But meat was not expected to think.

The second half of practice the meat squad scrimmaged the varsity. On offense he was cast as quarterback of the next opponent, Matawan or Point Pleasant, and whether handing off to a back, running the option, or dropping back to pass, he was leveled. Every play was the same play: the signal count, then soft crunch of shoulder pads, confused yells and grunts, then contact like the rush of a train, a distant whistle, and the quiet weight of bodies piled on top of him. It wasn't much different on defense, where he played cornerback. Billy Lewis, with a gang of blockers, was always bursting through a giant hole in the line and stampeding straight toward him. Maybe 5-8 and 140 pounds, he just toppled over backwards and reached up to grab feet and legs as they ran over his chest. Scrimmage offered the meat squad the pure experience of enduring blows.

When it grew dark, the team huddled around the coaches for strategy sessions, the meat squad at the margins, a ghostly irrelevance now. But sometimes they were summoned to take more. He remembered once, when the varsity was ordered back on the field to return kickoffs, he jogged down in coverage and was blind-sided by John Kunce, their finest 240-pound lineman. He lay on his back in the torn grass, never wanting to move, feeling the relief of the dead. When he opened his eyes, there was the towering figure of Coach Rosotti staring down at him. On his mafia face was a look of the most exquisite compassion. John was staring down as well, innocent and uncomprehending. It was the closest he had ever come to being welcomed into heaven.

Once practice was over, back in the locker room, all the pain was replaced by the deepest sense of solidarity he had known. For the meat squad, the challenge had been met and they were alive. Even the varsity players seemed to treat them like comrades in arms. The shower room, with its broken nozzles, chipped tiles, billows of steam, was abuzz with jokes and horseplay. Earl stood now under a shower talking with their team captain, Paul Dobrowski, a James Dean look-a-like, whose attentions kept the fawning lineman from realizing that the captain was pissing on his leg. For the meat squad, this was a restoration of justice. When he looked down, Earl jumped back, went berserk, and everyone broke up. They were inside the magic circle.

At the varsity games on Saturday afternoons, he would record all the plays on a clipboard from the sidelines. He also volunteered to tend to the injured. When Bobby Clark went down with a torn-up knee against Red Bank Catholic, he became the crutch helping him to the bench, where Bobby wept in pain amidst a litter of plastic cups, chewed orange rinds, and as the game went on, neglect. He remembered a brutal away game against Sayreville, played on a field that storms had turned into a prairie of mud and standing water. He watched as their backup defensive end, Rob Hamilton, entered the game in the second half wearing a clean uniform – sudden Technicolor in a world of indistinguishable brown shapes. No sign of transcendence, just an irresistible target for the Sayreville linemen, who jeered as he crouched into position. Rob came off the field a play later with his two upper front teeth knocked out. On the bus ride home, he sat next to Rob, mouth clamped into a blood-soaked towel.

He never did play varsity football at Rumson, because his family moved to Michigan his junior year. There he quarterbacked another high school team, until late that senior season his career ended the way John Kunce started it – a blind-side hit after the whistle, blowing out his knee. But that seemed fated too. He was still on the meat squad. Nothing quite matched the existential edge of being aligned with a hopeless cause, the voluntary martyrdom of joining it, the complex terms of surviving it. The experience was formative, and left him with an irrepressible, if distorted way of viewing events outside the chalk lines.

That same perspective resurfaced in his early twenties, and drew him into the civil rights struggle in the South. It began in Paris, reading in *The International Herald Tribune* of Michael Schwerner, James Chaney, and Andrew Goodman, an early meat squad from the Congress of Racial Equality, being murdered by the Klan in Mississippi. The moral rightness of this struggle was self-evident, with a clear underdog, an engagement no more complicated really than wanting to beat Sayreville. Only one injunction here: put your body on the line. Passive but resistant meat, something he understood. On the back steps of Brown's chapel the night before the march from Selma, keeping watch against marauding whites, an unloaded rifle on his lap. On the streets of Montgomery, arrested after being thrown through the glass window of a department store. On the sidewalks of Orangeburg, blocked by a giant barber with a razor, a Klansman without his hood, eyes glinting like two chinks of glass. None of this matched the terror of the Mississippi summer of 1964, but he suspected its leader, Bob Moses, put an end to the strategy when it became clear that someone on the meat squad, especially when white, became far more useful news when dead. But what he remembered most was the holy sense of community.

And then in his mid-twenties he signed up for Vietnam. Out of guilt? Simple curiosity? Death tripping? Bearing witness? Whatever, for almost a full tour he participated in what the U.S. military commanders called "search and destroy" missions, but were the opposite. Dump teenage grunts into the booby-trapped, mine-filled, guerrilla-controlled jungle, and once they were ambushed, call in the napalm. He had been an anti-war activist in the South, but realized only in the Central Highlands and Mekong Delta that the grunts of Vietnam were the tragic meat squad of his generation: brothers sacrificed for nothing, 58,000 of them, including Earl Scholl, one way or another *wasted, greased, iced,* their graphic language for death a reminder of their physical mortality, an antidote to the Orwellian lies that justified the invasion. As he saw it, the war came to an end only when the nation woke up in protest as white middle-class KIAs came back in body bags, and the meat squads in-country mutinied through drugs and fragging. But not for returning vets like himself. Twice as many had committed suicide after the war as were killed in Vietnam, as if in loyalty to fallen comrades, as if survival guilt could be purged by death alone.

He didn't go that far. He lost a leg, but he had volunteered to go, and his wound could be viewed as good luck given the circumstances. He leaned back on the sofa, scratching the end of his stump. He could see a member of any meat squad carried off a dangerous respect for loss, for what could success possibly mean now? Lethargy settled in that in his case bordered on immobilization. A sense of absence that is really loyalty to what has passed. Across the room from him, on a bookcase shelf was a framed picture of his mother. Last year he had leaned over her casket in Florida and kissed her cheek, firm and cold as marble. He had been away a year and a half and failed to reach her side in time. The same mother who, rightly fearful of meat squads, never grasped how her own innocent heart had inspired her children to volunteer. The same mother who, after dinner was over and his homework done, would apply sulfur compresses to the acne on his face and shoulders. The same mother who, every morning for the three months of the football season, was always there to help him out of bed he was so sore.

Twin

Down at the hospital, he says, too many of his patients refuse to die. Take old Mr. Solomon's tumor right now. It would win the Detroit grocer a blue ribbon at the State Fair. Two months ago it was a tiny rind. Now it pushes through his cheek like a stinking red cauliflower.

The two used to talk a lot, but now Mr. Solomon's moved on from Percodan to Dilaudid, spaced most of the time.

After a check-up at the diabetes clinic at Henry Ford, I find him in the burns ward, where Mr. Birsky sits behind drawn window blinds, a melted mound of flesh after failing into a lye vat at the Chrysler plant. Family visits ceased after a good look. Making new holes for his eyes, nose, and mouth, he says, was like carving a pumpkin. The ward fills up with an intimate silence as he brushes Mr. Birsky's teeth, toothpaste bubbling back into his cupped palm.

It's a routine by now, the two of us climbing to his attic on the third floor, rolling some joints, and me listening to him speak this way about pumpkins and cauliflower and blue ribbons – as if that foot in my face those roughhouse months in the womb was not the touch of love. I worry about his attachment to his patients. Maybe it's inflamed by his memories as a medic in Vietnam. He has not handled those well, locked up in a vault of silence. There was a Vietnamese girl burned by napalm, he says, whom he treated in Saigon, then quickly drops it. Yet he can't reign in his hatred for the American military brass he encountered there.

Now his outbursts are aimed at the gallery of Republican presidents, from Reagan to Trump, who have rolled back the '60s and enthroned wealth. But the outbursts have deeper origins. His first year as an intern at a hospital outside Portland, surgeons got hold of a hippie flower child with a stomach pain. They operated on her needlessly and she died. A girl, he says, he had fallen in love with, killed by her doctors as he wrote in the official hospital report. Appeals from the hospital administration couldn't pressure him to change a word. His internship was terminated.

Humans are just endorphin-crazed donkeys, he says. The country is wholesale into money and power, and minus that, pussy and drugs. He says it could be worse. Take countries like apartheid South Africa, where someone comes and simply takes away your kids. How would you deal with that? When it did happen to me, losing my sons in a custody battle in the Detroit courts, he stares out the attic window. Share with me, he says, his dream of Rebecca dead, her limbs scattered up and down the street so they can be routinely run over driving through the neighborhood. Listening to him is like listening to a secret self, one as real as what I offer to the world, which I keep at the far edge of consciousness.

Venting his opinion on public issues offers him some release from the suffering of his patients, however grim or lunatic those opinions might be. The pharmaceuticals, he says, have the medical profession by the balls, either buying them off or offering them all the free Percodan they want, leaving a quarter of the doctors in the country addicted. He will turn to international affairs, remembering the strange things Noriega kept under his dresser – dirty magazines, chicken hearts, a bottle of nipples. Or switch to presidents, picking off the signs of Reagan's dementia, how Iran-Contra occurred without him knowing a thing. Or even airlines, how People's Express lets you know too much, announcing the plane is being towed to the gate, was nicked on the tarmac by a baggage truck, or is leaving a holding pattern for a nearby airport because it's running out of fuel.

I might laugh, but uneasily, recognizing that all of these opinions, whether serious or not, reveal a resistant black humor that assumes the omnipresence of sudden death.

But apart from offering company, there is little I can do because his dream life is the problem. I may have a similar one, provoked by the whole blood-soaked century, but the difference is in the details. His day ends with all his patients lined up for emergency visits. After the swimming pool has been cleaned, the garden weeded, the kids played with and put to bed. All the metaphors tucked away. Then, falling asleep into a realm of twins, he steps forward to embrace the life, ward off the death.

Hereafter

I was standing in a checkout line at Kroger's, watching the woman ahead of me unwrap a slab of sirloin from butcher paper and slam the meat on the scales at the counter. She was menacing the sad-faced Hispanic woman working the register. "Weigh this again!" she demanded. "Those guys in the meat department are trying to cheat me!" The woman had the shape and complexion of a pale pink roast, her blue eyes flashing wildly from two cups of flab.

"You shouldn't be so cross with her," came a soft voice from behind. I turned. It was a teenage girl, dwarfed by a burly man standing next to her. He wore a Detroit Tigers cap that drew attention to his huge, wrinkled neck. She was skinny, with colorless blonde hair, and had the same receding chin as the man, who I assumed was her father.

"You shut your fuckin' mouth," he barked at her suddenly. "Stay out of other people's business! Ain't you learned nothin'?"

The girl pointed her open hand toward the Hispanic woman at the register, now tense and cowering. "Don't you think," she said in a pleading tone, "she deserves to be treated with respect?"

"There you go again . . . Don't talk back to me!"

Without warning the burly man struck the girl square in the face with his fist. Then he pushed through the checkout line and stomped out the glass entrance doors. Shoppers stood there shocked. I was more primed, having passed the two of them in an aisle just five minutes ago, where I had happened to notice him snatch a can of fruit juice and gulp it down, then replace the empty can back on the shelf.

The girl lay on the cement floor, blood flowing from her nose and brow. Her eyes were glassy as they turned toward the ceiling as if searching for a message from God. The woman ahead of me wrapped up her meat and followed the Tiger cap out the entrance doors.

I dropped to a knee and lifted the girl's neck off the cement with my hand, then placed her head in the cradle of my forearm. Her green eyes wandered upon my face. "Thank you, " she murmured. "I'm afraid . . ." I touched her brow and kept holding her for a long while, with no impulse to move. She was innocent and defenseless, and it was obvious that was not going to change soon. Another shopper bent over us with concern, but I signaled her away. Time moved into another realm. I had not a grain of religious faith, but the flow of compassion coursing through me at that moment was too powerful to be my own.

If there were a hereafter it would start like this.

Pot Plantation

He was a TA in the English Department at UC-Berkeley finishing up his doctorate when he was drawn back into the drug trade. He started growing marijuana in a rented apartment in South San Francisco. It was very profitable until the landlord turned on him. Banner headlines in the *San Francisco Chronicle* read: "UC Grad Student Busted for Indoor Pot Plantation." His mug shot was shown beneath the thick letters, looking sheepish, despite the roguish mop of hair.

He was in serious trouble. A federal law was on the books, mandating a 20-year minimum sentence without parole for selling or growing any amount of marijuana. A respected professor in the English Department put him in touch with a group of liberal lawyers fighting these draconian sentences. One of them took his case, pro bono, and got him charged with violating a California state law, not a federal one. He was taken from the slammer at San Bruno, not a place you'd want to be, and sentenced to a year of overnights in San Francisco's new prison.

Life grew more complex. During the day he taught a composition class and did scholarly research on *The Faerie*

Queene. Then he drove across the Oakland-Bay Bridge in the evening, arriving at 6:00 sharp to spend the night. It was a super hi-tech prison, the cells pie-shaped and stacked in columns, with surveillance cameras everywhere. Loudspeakers barked out how to live your life twenty-four hours a day.

The first night he found out that psychodrama was used as a way to control aggression. He was the only white man among the new inmates, and once they were herded into an interrogation room, was destined to play Bernard Goetz, who had shot four young blacks mugging him on a New York City subway several years back. Three guards in blue uniforms were leaning against the pale green walls, huge arms across their chests. An old-timer in loose orange prison garb, his black face finely wrinkled under a shock of frizzled gray hair, observed from a distance. The inmates were instructed to improvise, reenact how they might have managed aggressive feelings more reasonably than Bernard Goetz had. But in truth he was the only one required to improve on history, since he was the perp.

He might have given it a try if he hadn't eavesdropped five minutes earlier on the two young blacks cast as the muggers on the subway. They had been arrested for almost killing some white guy behind a gas station, and he heard one of them bragging about it. "Shit, we started beatin' on that motherfucker just before midnight and didn't let up until an hour later. Fuck, man, you could say we was beatin' on that dude for two days!"

When the reenactment began, the two of them walked over to him seated on a bench. They started unloading a lot of threatening jive-ass bullshit. They seemed in heaven, incredulous, instructed to curse the white man in prison and get high marks for it. He said nothing, just stared at them, listening. Then he rose slowly, facing them, and making a pistol out of his right hand, pressed his forefinger to the temple of one and uttered succinctly: "BANG!" Then the second one, "BANG!" Inmates standing around watching were stunned. Then several applauded, and a few others came over to clap him on the shoulder, including the old-timer.

"You got that right, son," he said. "Can't talk yo' way out of every fuckin' scrape. Sometimes jus' gotta pick up the gun. Color ain't got nothin' to do with it."

Things settled down after the first night. He could not believe the young men that filled the prison. Buff, violent, their bodies covered with tattoos, knife scars, bullet wounds. They struck him as conscience-free killers, loyal to no one but members of their own gang. They existed outside the law. But he curbed any curiosity about their world, which he had passed through on occasion. He was more worried about any reputation he might have gained in the prison as the next Bernard Goetz. He hung with the older prisoners, kept quiet, compliant, staying as invisible as possible.

Seven months later he was allowed to sleep again on the other side of the Bay and focus upon *The Faerie Queene*.

Cardinal

The pine tree outside my window looks blue against the snow, and silence catches in its branches like invisible ice. It is so still my mind is pure observation. The shadow beneath the tree is a round gray light, enough to make the trunk look bolted to the ground. It's not going anywhere, just there, stunning in its integrity. In front of the pine tree, nearer the window, is a young maple. It's naked of leaves, with lithe silver branches rising in the air like antlers, alert, sampling the air, radiating a future.

A male cardinal lands on a branch of the maple. Its brilliant red crest and chest are a celestial ornament against the backdrop of pine tree and snow. Its orange beak, protruding from a black facemask, seems momentarily comical, but fades back into mystery. A second cardinal arrives on the branch, a brown female, then another male. They stare at me through the window, taking my measure, refusing to fly away. They find me acceptable. I can't remember ever having experienced such a feeling before.

When I look away, then back out the window, the three cardinals are gone. I feel like all the birds in the world have flown away. Imagining such a loss is crushing. The absence of that incessant chatter in the air, barely heard, yet full of life's energies – courtship, temper tantrums, playfulness, family politics, pure song. Silence reasserts itself in the pine tree, and the idea of its permanence fills me with dread.

The cardinal revisits me in a dream. I'm looking out the same window, but it is no longer standing on the branch of the maple but closer, on the outside windowsill. It is huge. I press my face up to the pane and look into the cardinal's eyes. Black marbles, lidless, perfectly round, the crest above them a pointed red flame. In those eyes I see my reflection. It's daunting, but I see love there and press my cheek against the windowpane. The bird presses his giant chest against the glass, as if trying to reach me, before flying off into a burst of sunlight.

Black Lava

The moon was full and Scott's pockets filled with joints that spring night they walked over to Steve Williams' house. He lived a couple of tree-lined blocks away from Larry's own new rental in a northwest Dayton neighborhood. In his early thirties, Steve was a colleague in the English department down at Wright State, a light-skinned black man, with a pencil mustache, as handsome and debonair as a Motown vocalist. He had published a few novels. Larry didn't really know him, but Scott had regarded his invite to drop over as full of visionary possibility, at least privileged access to the city's creative elite. The two went back to Berkeley days, so Larry had seen him wrap himself in the shroud of universal brotherhood and slip below the surface before.

Steve greeted them on the porch of a modest Tudor on Renfrew and led them down into a furnished basement. Two black men were seated on a lumpy couch under the low ceiling. Rich was tall and muscular, his square shoulders bursting from under a maroon pullover. He looked sleek and intuitive in a pair of expensive slacks. More casually dressed, Russell was even taller, high yellow, gawky, with big hands and a wide, insulting stare. Larry sensed a latent violence in the basement that seemed to turn the air glutinous. There were perfunctory introductions, drinks made, joints passed, eddies of disconnected laughter.

Rich turned to focus on Larry. "So you teach with Steve, that right?"

"Right, just started my first year at Wright State."

"Where'd you come from?"

"California."

"You leave there for here? Sheeit! Where'bouts?"

"Berkeley."

"Whoa! All those hippie chicks into free love, right? They puttin' out for everybody?"

"Not exactly. What do you do?"

"I was one of the meanest college cornerbacks who never make the NFL."

"No kidding. What about now?"

"CPA. I'm a financial advisor, a walking tax loophole. How 'bout you? You got any money to play with?"

Larry smiled and raised his hands in surrender. "No, no action here. With teaching, you know, it's hand-to-mouth . . ."

Rich seemed to lose interest. Instead he stood up and strode around the basement, pausing before a poster of Malcolm X over the shallow, green-tiled fireplace. Then he started to deliver forearm shivers to ghost opponents, stopping just short of striking a floor lamp, just grazing the cinderblock walls.

Larry shifted his attention to Scott, who was catching a lot of ridicule and intimidation from the other man, Russell.

"What do you teach, Ruhlman? Santa Claus?"

Scott laughed in a conciliatory way, tugging at his beard, but Russell kept it up. "Are you a hippie? What you gonna teach my kids? Say somethin' . . . *Say somethin'!*"

"To tell the truth, Russell, I'm just a frog on a lily pad in the middle of the pond, snapping at flies and whatever else comes by."

"You ain't calling me a fuckin' fly, are you?"

Steve appeared before them from the margins. "You jiving us, right, Russell?" He was acting like some puppet master in charge, exuding camaraderie, but chuckling to himself. Suddenly he looked with admiration at his friend, whispering under his breath, "How long you gonna sit there and play the devil's game?"

Russell stood up now, towered over Scott, who was nursing a joint with a spacy, worried look on his face.

"Know how I get off, Ruhlman? I go out in my back yard with my machine gun and fire clips at the moon. That's what I like to do. What you gotta say about that?"

Scott looked academic, helpless.

"That's how all those holes got in that cheese," Rich added dryly.

Larry had tolerated about enough when Russell suddenly turned to him. "How 'bout you? Say something!"

He was tongue-tied.

"Know what I like about Tokyo Rose?" Russell announced to the basement walls. "She wanted to liquidate America. Now that's a program I respect."

The hatred in his voice was tangible, like sound blisters. Larry looked away and noticed for the first time two other black men in the far corner of the basement, one bearded and in a jump suit, the other wearing a pith helmet, grinning. He was tense with anger the way Scott was being treated, so vulnerable in his pained sincerity.

Then Russell pressed his face close to his. "What do you teach?"

"Back off, man. How about you?" Russell was all lip and teeth. "My next-door neighbor is a vet, ready to leave Dayton for Montana because he's sick of digging bullets out of dogs. Is that your line of work?"

"Don't get cute with me, motherfucker . . ."

Russell lunged at him but stumbled over the coffee table, and Larry checked throwing a punch at his exposed head. Then Steve was posted between the two, laughing, as if he were watching a harmless joust, the antics of a weird friend. "Everything's cool, men," he said. "I got it all on tape. This is good material."

Material? Steve made clear what the evening was about by going over to an end table by the couch and clicking off a tape recorder. As if on cue, his two friends stood up and left without a word, Rich leading Russell up the stairs like a circus animal, a sinister vaudeville team.

"Yeah, Larry, this is how I do my writing. It's the real thing. Listen, I just got a story here I want you and Scott to hear. Any critical suggestions would be appreciated."

Steve pulled a manuscript from a nearly table drawer and started to read aloud, a slang-ridden exchange between two drug dealers in the Morton corridor, near Wright State. Was this a transcribed tape? Anger and depression started to wilt Larry as he swept long black hair off his face. This was just bad acid, these faces, the fake fireplace, the two guys in jump suit and pith helmet still grinning in the corner, the rough surface of cinderblock showing through the green wall paint.

It was time for some fresh air. Larry managed to get Scott off the couch, genuinely disoriented, as if he didn't realize that a slug was resting in his gut. Larry had no heart to confront Steve, who was all brotherly love as he waved them into darkness from his driveway.

Just how to react when confronted by a homicidal case like Russell was unresolved. No disgrace there. Yet Larry had swallowed a lot of fear and rage, an unmanning experience. But it was more Steve Williams' deviousness that impressed him as they walked back in the night. At the least, what happened was staged, a racist psychodrama, with his friend offered up as white meat to feed the tape. He had been used as a means, and the hell with hurt feelings. The hell with any consequences for that matter. What happened in the basement touched upon a lot of dark impulses, including murder.

"I'd say we just got trashed, Scott."

"I was confused most of the time, stoned, but there was black rage in the air. That Russell was a nutcase."

"Wasn't this supposed to be an opportunity to meet Dayton's black literary scene?"

A corner streetlight revealed dog shit on the sidewalk. Larry skipped over it.

Gorillas

A ten-year-old boy stared at the cartoon on the huge TV screen at Best Buy. A gorilla was running through the jungle, pulling up trees and grabbing natives along the way, throwing his captives up into the air to disappear into undergrowth. There were no screams, no one hurt. The gorilla didn't appear mean. It was a typical gorilla face, handsome when you accepted it, and a set of shoulders that he had only seen in Superhero comics. He left a good impression, maybe because of the playful havoc he was wrecking in the jungle. The boy imagined them being friends.

He saw his first live gorilla at the Bronx zoo, through the bars of a cage. The silverback turned his back and cast a baleful look over his shoulder. Soon a gang of teenage boys drifted by and started yelling at the gorilla. A redhead began to throw pebbles at him through the bars, intended to hurt. Moving with startling speed, the gorilla scraped up what looked like vomit off the cement floor of his cage and threw it at them. Promptly a zoo attendant in white overalls appeared to escort the boys to the front gates.

He lingered by the cage. The gorilla calmed down. Maybe this one wasn't as outgoing as the one in the cartoon, but he could understand why. He admired the way the imprisoned creature tried to drive off those jerks. Maybe the gorilla had snubbed him earlier thinking he was like them. Already he saw the two of them as friends.

The following summer he came upon a cardboard box in the attic filled with his father's collection of old Tarzan comics. Immediately he devoured them. He learned through wondrous artful illustrations that Tarzan was born to British aristocrats who had become marooned in equatorial Africa. When a renegade tribe of great apes killed them, Kala, a she-ape, raised their infant, who grew up to become lord of the jungle. He came to love Tarzan's friends, Tantor the elephant, Numa the lion, and Sheeta the panther as much as he did the handsome, white-skinned, loin-clothed youth who swung through trees as if flung from a slingshot. If he had been nurtured and protected by gorillas, that was evidence enough. Their nobility was established beyond any doubt. The familial merging of these two species in Tarzan comics planted in him a keen awareness of the kinship between all living animals.

By high school he had learned everything about gorillas, their gentleness, vegetarianism, and love for their young. These were virtues he would adopt as his own as a grown-up. The silverback roaring and beating his chest was largely a bluff, creating just enough fear to ward off any physical clash. He was amazed to find out gorillas were the exact opposite of what people thought. Then one day, watching a documentary on Netflix, he learned how they were being wiped out in Africa. He was devastated. Native poachers were killing them for bush meat, selling their paws for ashtrays, and cutting off their heads for trophies to hang in the dens of rich people around the world. It was his first gut-check with reality. Still he fought back, telling his friends about their plight and volunteering his weekends at animal rescue shelters.

In college, during his junior year abroad, he went to Rwanda to search out the mountain gorillas. One day, hiking alone, he turned a bend in the trail and came upon a large female resting on a grassy bank. He froze, but was not afraid as she advanced and wrapped her arms around him, leaving the fog of her breath on his glasses before disappearing back into the jungle.

Years later he was sitting in his living room with his five-year-old son. They were watching the original black-and-white movie of "King Kong" on TV. Early on the great ape, having taken his promised sacrifice, Fay Wray, back into the interior of Skull Island, is attacked by a tyrannosaurus rex.

"Why are they fighting each other?" the boy cried out.

"Well, it's just the nature of monsters."

"Why is the girl afraid of King Kong?"

"She thinks he's going to harm her. She doesn't

understand that King Kong likes her."

His son paused. "Know what, Dad? King Kong can't talk!"

When the movie was ending, his wife came downstairs and the three went out for a Buddy's pizza. On the drive there, Rowan could not stop talking about what he had just seen. "Mom, there's another King Kong, a real nice one who doesn't get in fights. He lives with us. He doesn't do any of those things on TV. He has white hands with fingernail polish and he brings me cookies . . . He doesn't like girls, either!"

He had to smile. His son, having discovered the wonders of fingernail polish last week, had at one stroke domesticated King Kong and turned him into a friend.

At Buddy's, with his face smeared with pizza toppings, the boy reviewed for his parents the highlights of the movie in great detail. How King Kong saved the girl from the giant python, then the huge pterodactyl. "Every time King Kong was nice to the girl, Mom, they hurt him." Or how once captured, the great ape was brought to America in chains, put on a stage for audiences to gape and tremble at, now reduced from a god to a sideshow. "Mom, they made fun of King Kong and scared him. Then he saw the girl in the audience and broke free to be with her." Most upsetting to the boy was how the behemoth, after reaching what should have been freedom, the top of the Empire State Building, was machine-gunned by gnat-like

121

bi-planes and fell to his death. "That was sad," Rowan sighed, "because King Kong just wanted to go home, not be in a movie."

His son didn't realize there was no longer any home for gorillas that was safe. After putting him to bed, he stood on the front porch looking down the darkened street. He had mixed emotions. That gorillas had captured Rowan's imagination, as they had his own when he was young, was reassuring. Yet it was an ambivalent legacy. Gorillas would be extinct within a decade, and what then? He had read about the silence that fell upon the English countryside when all their livestock were slaughtered to stem an epidemic of Mad Cow Disease. And when the gorillas were gone? Their silence, interrupted by ghostly snorts and happy labored breathing, would probably reside in his mind forever.

The Substitute

Elaine picked up the small gray sweatshirt, now sleeveless, and took the scissors from his hand.

"You're not making good choices, Anthony."

She had been having trouble with the four-year-old. He seemed disabled in some way. His tangled black hair stood up on his head like he was being electrocuted.

"Now let's practice letters. Do you have an 'A' in your name?"

No response. But by now silence was welcome. The boy had been screaming, loud and often, and for no reason that Elaine could make out. Earlier that morning screams from other children had gone off like cherry bombs in other parts of the classroom, but they had subsided.

"Too bad it's snowing, isn't it, Anthony? Tomorrow we can go outside if the snow stops and practice pumping on the swings."

His eyes widened with alarm. "No . . . we can't go outside."

This was Elaine's second day as a substitute teacher here and she had forgotten. The ten children, two whites and the rest black or Hispanic, were assigned to this classroom for seven hours with no cafeteria break, no gym, and no recess. No matter how many toys, crayons, brightly colored chalkboards there might be, it was still a lockdown.

"It's for the good of the children," Karen, the obese black teacher in charge, had told her yesterday. "They might run home, or just run away."

The pre-school, funded by a federal grant, was attached to an old brick elementary school in a run-down neighborhood of Ypsilanti. The area was bordered by a long strip of junk-food restaurants, liquor stores, a Dollar store, a Wal-Mart, used-car lots, the usual rural Midwestern wasteland.

"Gramma Delane, will you rub my back like yesterday?"

The boy lay down on the floor, hopeful.

"During nap time, Anthony. I promise."

The children called Elaine that because she was sixty-six, twice as old as most of the other female teachers moving in and out of the classroom. She had been a successful self-employed art appraiser for thirty years in Chicago, smart and attractive. Before that was chaos. As a teenager she had run away from home, pregnant, and had a back-alley abortion in Portland that left her unable to conceive again. Losing the chance to raise a child left her with a permanent, though marginal sense of alienation from the future. She was now back in Michigan where she was born, her parents deceased, living alone in an apartment with no pension and few prospects.

Karen walked over and squatted. "Elaine, please don't get on the floor with the children. It gets too chaotic. Would you assemble them around the mystery bag so they can take turns describing and guessing what objects are in there?"

She rose, a little irked by these directions. Why couldn't she get down with the children? Why was this staff teacher so jealous of their attraction to her? Elaine had been dismissed from an Ann Arbor school she was substituting at last month for drinking from a bottle of water that was meant for snails in an aquarium. And a second school had dismissed her for sharing her ham sandwich with a child because he was allergic to peanut butter. It was absurd.

She found the mystery bag, lumpish and white, resting by the bookcase, and called the children over. Nisaiah, Jaccari, Anthony, Messiah, Zayla, Tyrone, Brooklyn, Serenity, Brandon, and Alisa. Names she had memorized yesterday because she immediately liked them: their faces, expressions, quirks, sense of humor . . . their astonishing *newness*. She picked up the fear in their irrational hesitations and sudden caution, as if some threat were hanging over them. They took turns pulling items out of the bag – plastic dinosaurs, trucks, dolls, an assortment of balls, rubber-dart guns, cards – items that seemed of timeless interest to children.

"All right, it's nap time," Karen spoke up, her voice stern but tender. The children got out mats and placed them on the floor. Some were quiet, some noisy, with a few screamers starting up again, including Anthony. Elaine moved over from Serenity and lay down beside him. She started rubbing his back, calming him. The room grew quiet as the two spoke in whispers.

"What did you get out of the mystery bag, Anthony?"

"A dinosaur. They breathe fire and can tear down towers. People are scared of them but they like me."

"Did you know that the dinosaurs all died a long time ago when a big rock hit the earth?"

"No . . . I don't like that story."

"No, of course not. I'm sorry."

"Do you know why I cry a lot, Gramma Delane? Because I like school and know I have to go home. I can't go outside. My dad is mean. He hits Mommy and me."

Karen came by and asked them to stop whispering.

That afternoon the classroom hummed with activities. Elaine read to Messiah, Zayla, and Brooklyn from Ellen Stoll Walsh's *Mouse Paint*. There was a puppet show and Karen brought play dough out to place on the tables. Several children helped water one of the classroom plants, and then sketched it in their journals. Others made shapes, lines, and letters on Geo Boards. They played games of "In and Out of the Square" and "In and Out of Hula Hoops," then a beanbag toss.

Then another nap before the day ended.

Elaine drove home, exhausted. A twenty-minute trip back

into Ann Arbor. Whatever complaints she had about the day were outweighed by her fondness for the children. Their remarks were so spontaneous and funny, so unpredictable. And those names! What were the parents thinking of? What was wrong with normal American names? Just posing the question to herself provided the answer. What had normal America, with its prejudice against ethnic minorities, now bred in the bone, ever offered them? These children were all originals, some smart, others not, with most of them waging a brave struggle against the odds. Even pre-school opportunities like this hardly gave them a chance.

Elaine prepared that evening for the next day's class, sitting next to a gas fireplace in a silent apartment. She had checked out some children's books from the Ann Arbor library in search of some better choices to read aloud. She prepared a dozen sheets of paper to play tic-tac-toe tomorrow. She took one sheet and made little ink drawings of the children in the nine squares.

Going to bed early, she missed a late email telling her that her services would not be needed the next day. She read it at 6:30 in the morning while getting ready to drive to the school. She was angry. She could see a heavy snowfall outside the window and knew they had scratched her because there would be low attendance. The school could save some money, but not much, because her pay for seven hours of teaching was $70.

Her experience had been that substitute teachers were

treated like dirt.

But she was fortunate in this instance. She was in a coffee shop late that afternoon, and picked up a late edition of *The Detroit News*. Headlines read of a shooting at the pre-school. Three children were dead, and there were photographs of them. One was one of Anthony, smiling broadly. Karen had been shot and was in critical condition. Anthony's father had entered the building that noon with a gun, wearing a mask and camouflage, drunk or high on something. The last one he shot before himself was his son. The motive was still speculation, but apparently neo-Nazi white supremacist literature was found in his trailer. A neighbor told police the man was crazy, a meth freak who believed schools were teaching children to hate whites and favor blacks.

Elaine was devastated. Anthony, Messiah, Zayla, gone. Others hurt.

That night she dreamed of the classroom as if she had gone to work that morning. Everyone was present. The usual activities were going on. The children seemed in a good mood, no one screaming. Enough snow had fallen to leave the windows a white glaze. She was extraordinarily lively in her participation in the activities. Molding the play dough into a circus of little animals that delighted them, playing endless games of tic-tac-toe, riding an overwhelming current of maternal love. Then a long nap time when she rubbed the back of each child. No one woke up.

Swish

When I was thirteen in Toledo, a friend and I were high up in a tree, on a branch overhanging a residential street, dropping chunks of watermelon onto the roofs of passing cars. I lost my grip and fell. I saw Paul's shocked face distancing itself from me as I banged through branches and hit the sidewalk hard. Before I passed out I already knew something new: no feeling in my legs.

In the eighth grade then, I had a crush on a pretty, freckle-faced blond girl who was aware of my furtive glances, yet never returned them. Mary was shy. But when I returned to school in a wheelchair, to the surprise and curiosity of many, she turned her attention on me more earnestly than I could have ever dreamed of earlier. It was because of the accident. I assumed she felt sorry for me, though I was good-looking enough and popular, an A student like herself. I could get around school on my own, my arms weren't paralyzed, but she placed herself in charge of the wheelchair. She pushed me down noisy hallways to classes. She was around when I watched recess, which was painful since I loved sports and had been a good athlete. I told her how I used to practice basketball in my basement, dribbling around traffic cones with black tape over the lower half of my glasses, to develop control of the ball without looking down. She seemed perplexed, but still escorted me not only to classes, but assemblies, pep rallies, class picnics, fire drills, the whole deal. In the course of her performing these charities, something happened. Mary and I got to know each other deeply and fell into an adolescent, but genuine kind of love that was new to both of us.

We moved on to Roosevelt High where we remained inseparable, except when Mary was at some girls' club, playing soccer, or doing gymnastics. She might have had some dates, although I never saw her with another guy. I had erotic emotions but couldn't even masturbate. The prospect of a future without sex left me feeling depressed and abandoned. I had lost what I would never have the chance to even experience. But Mary was still present, literally and spiritually. She encouraged me to work out in the weight room, keep my upper body strong, and I followed her advice. But being crippled put me in another category. I was cut off from much of teenage life – all the mischief, horsing around, prowling for adventure and sex. And I would never play the sports I had dreamed of playing in high school.

Instead Mary persuaded me to run for student council president my junior year. Friends rallied to the idea, and she ran my campaign that spring. Mustaches appeared on the hallway posters of the incumbent, Buddy Dodd, class president since ninth grade. I was the wild card candidate in a wheelchair and benefited from that. Being paralyzed stirred empathy in people that could override everything else. And there were plenty in our class getting tired of Buddy. At a school assembly before the election, I wheeled myself out onto the stage and made dubious promises about getting senior class rings early, publishing a student directory useful for dating, and other inanities. I won in a landslide.

Mary didn't stop there. At her insistence I enrolled in a radical medical research study on the treatment of spinal injuries underway at Ohio State hospitals. She had learned they were experimenting with stem cell injection therapy. I read articles on the research, and she even drove me to Columbus in a new Subaru van that her parents had bought her. That it was equipped with a lift for wheelchair-bound passengers astonished me. Rising on the lift for the first time, I realized she was unwilling to leave me behind. Even to the extent of holding out hope for some miracle of physical rehabilitation. She was very determined, more than I was, like her own future depended on it.

Another kind of miracle happened my senior year. I was in the gym, my wheelchair parked against the bleachers, watching Roosevelt High's basketball team in a final practice before the state playoffs started. I was waiting for Mary to emerge from the locker room after gymnastics to take me home.

"Hi."

Her face peeked around from behind my shoulder. A lovely young woman now, still freckled, in sleek athletic shape. I could smell her skin and felt a stir of sensation in my lower body. When practice was over, as Mary wheeled me across the court toward the exit, a stray basketball rolled up against my chair. I reached down and picked it up. With the hoop sticking out from the glass backboard maybe ten feet away, I flung the basketball in that direction in a kind of hook shot. It swished.

"Hey, pretty good." Mary stopped to retrieve the basketball and came back. "Here, try that again."

This time I wheeled myself back to the three-point line, placed both hands on the ball, and took a set shot. Swish.

Mary stood there, flabbergasted, as I took shot after shot. Swish. Swish. I never missed. A few players leaving the gym stopped to watch, incredulous. Then the lights dimmed, and everyone left, leaving just the fading echo of bouncing basketballs in an empty gym.

On the drive home, Mary asked over her shoulder, "Craig, what happened just now?"

"All I know is that when I shot that basketball there was no doubt it was going in. It was like dropping clothespins into a pail. And there was something else. It felt like I was easing all the pain and loss from the accident . . . Every swish was a flash of hope, a new beginning . . ."

At school the next morning I was called to the office of Mr. Harmon, our Driver Ed instructor, who also coached the basketball team. Hair covered his skull like a thick black tire tread. He said some players had watched me in the gym yesterday. He asked me to come to practice that afternoon. He looked at me oddly, as the whole student body often looked oddly at him. It was an open secret Mr. Harmon was meeting with Ms. Delano, an English teacher, in the gym's laundry room behind locked doors. He had four kids at home.

"Sure, Mr. Harmon. I'll be there."

Mary was free to get me to the gym. Basketballs stopped bouncing on the hardwood when I arrived, and players moved to the edges of the court. Mr. Harmon was all business, pushing my wheelchair to the foul line facing the basket, and then placing a basketball in my lap.

"Okay, Craig, let's see if it's true what the team is saying about you."

The gym grew quiet, but alert. I bounced the basketball on the hardwood. There was a small balcony behind the glass backboard and I could see Mary up there, seated alone in a row of bleachers. I shot and the basketball swished through the net. Then another shot, another swish, again and again. The ball never touched the rim, just the net which itself barely moved. After a dozen shots, Mr. Harmon pulled my wheelchair back to the three-point line.

"Let's see what you can do from here." Five, a dozen,

two dozen swishes. I never missed. "Okay, that's enough."

Mr. Harmon walked toward me looking puzzled, as if he had just witnessed either a remarkable shooting exhibition or freak show, and wasn't sure which. But the players were sure. They crowded around my wheelchair, patting me on the shoulders, offering congratulations. They knew exactly the improbability of what they had just seen.

"Coach," one spoke up, "we could use Craig on the team for the playoffs." Another yelled, "Right on!" Tom Evans, the team captain, agreed. "Coach, Craig is already our student council president. Why not Roosevelt's three-point-shooting guard?"

By the time the state playoffs started, I was officially on the basketball team. After a special session, Ohio's high school athletic association allowed me to play using a motorized wheelchair with hand controls. I got lucky. It was now politically correct to include the handicapped in as many student activities as possible.

In the early games I played sparingly. Obviously a liability on defense, except as a screen or some intractable obstacle interrupting the flow. I came in for a quarter, but my time on the court increased as we kept winning, with me parked behind the three-point line and swishing any shots I was able to get off. My teammates knew I wouldn't miss, didn't have to worry about offensive rebounds since there weren't any. They just set up two and three-man screens to give me a chance to shoot. By the time we advanced to the quarterfinals, scouting reports had singled me out as a genuine offensive threat. The swarming defense our opponents imposed on me the next two games only left my teammates open, and we made it to the final.

The day the team boarded a bus for the arena in Columbus, I saw Mary in the hallway. "I feel anxious," I told her. "Something's different. During this run I've never had any mental static, any doubt about my shots going in. Now the confidence isn't there. And my toes tingle."

She stared at me, looked around, and then kissed me lightly on the lips. Without a word she walked down the hallway, smiling back.

Devilbus High, wearing orange and black, was an excellent team. Tall, fast, and undefeated. We stayed close to them in the first half, helped by several three-pointers I converted through a thicket of converging arms. They double-teamed me in the second half, grabbing onto the wheels of my chair to impede me, but that left them vulnerable elsewhere. Tom Evans went on a torrid shooting streak, leaving us down by two points with half a minute to play. Devilbus was running out the clock when our point guard made a steal under our basket, stood up, and threw a full-court pass to me racing into our offensive zone in the wheelchair.

The arena was in an uproar. The pass was too long for me to reach. Instinctively I rose up and grabbed it out of the air, sending the empty wheelchair rolling out of bounds. I turned and let go a three-point shot. It arched high in the air and tracking it I could see an empty row of seats in the balcony with a single figure watching. The basketball hit the rim, rattled around, and bounced out. The game was over. I was crestfallen, still unaware that I was standing on my feet like any other player, with no guarantee every shot would go in.

But the entire arena, packed with fans from both schools, just continued to shout and applaud with an energy that would not quit.

Listening

He walked into the room as if it promised him a lover, but instead his friends were discussing him as if he were absent and could only materialize in their words. He stood inside the door, undetected, listening in silence, with an eager and helpless kind of curiosity as they gathered around a dim lamp in the corner. Their words sounded crude and preliminary to his ears, often misleading put next to his own bouts of introspection. Still, he continued to listen, for somehow it was their testimony alone that mattered now. Soon he recognized that they read selfishness in his actions that he would never have expected of them. In their eyes, his ambivalent traits did not hold in suspension any imminent virtue. Even his own passion for clarity was viewed as a false impulse, not close to the heart of things at all. Finally his unfailing pleasantness was challenged, stripped away as regulated rage and defense by voices whose lives, he surmised, were also in ruins. All of this took ingenious expansion until he could imagine himself as some skeleton floating in a cauldron of acid. Still there was the compulsion to listen in silence, like a criminal who returns to the scene of the crime out of loneliness.

He listened to other voices from his past that started to speak inside his head. There was his father denouncing his ingratitude and unpatriotic political realignments. There was his ex-wife scoring his infidelities and addictions. There was his beloved son telling him that all his early success and honors as a medical researcher had happened despite him, by ignoring his example. There was a brilliant college professor who had turned him from physics to literature saying that his writing was not what he had expected or hoped for at all. He heard African-American voices dismissing the arrests and beatings he endured in the civil rights struggle as just some guilt-laced narcissism exploiting their suffering. He had what he felt were reasonable defenses against all these indictments, but the voices were bodiless, had no ears for listening. While his ears had grown into gigantic rubbery flaps that heard everything, twitching like an elephant's.

A characteristic movement at such a moment is to recline on the floor and deliciously stretch out your limbs, then feel them contract like slowly burning paper.

Freaks

A pale blue sky arched over the Michigan State Fair as
Doug and his son passed through the entrance gates. Theo
was seven, wearing new orange sneakers. The smell of
fried corn dogs reached them from a nearby cluster of food
wagons. They had crossed over Woodward Avenue from
their neighborhood to take in the sights. Acres of rides and
booths spread out before them in inviting confusion. Theo
broke away, skipping on ahead until he came upon an exhibit framed by a banner reading in red script: Dunk Bozo.

"Dad, can I play this?" He stepped up to a wooden railing and reached into a trough of stained baseballs, under
the watchful eye of Bozo, who sat ten yards away on a
plank suspended over a tub of water.

"Lookit those ears! You little brat. Where'd you get that
ugly shirt? From a dumpster?"

It was Theo's favorite shirt, pale yellow speckled with
blue parrots. He was quite handsome, with pale blue eyes
and a halo of blond hair, but was sensitive about his ears.
He was thrown off balance by the insults, a weak smile
pasted on his lips.

"Go ahead, kiddo. You know how to shut Bozo up."

"Lookit Dad there. Needs some Vitalis, don't he? Looks like he's wearing a mop on his head . . ."

The small gathering of onlookers chuckled. Throwing an arm out, Doug bowed and smiled, while Theo was sizing up the challenge. He had three baseballs to throw at the target, a circular wooden bull's-eye attached to a lever positioned to the right of Bozo. The teenager was garbed in long underwear with red and blue stripes. An accurate throw would unhook the plank and plunge him into the water.

"Com'on, little brat, throw it. You retarded? That hippo behind you wants a turn. Who're you, Dad? Think you're Einstein, with that hair? An' those eyes, Jesus . . . close 'em before you bleed to death!"

Bozo was good, Doug thought. The bloodshot eyes were chronic. He looked down at his son and saw he was misty-eyed. But Theo had a rifle for an arm. He threw twice and missed, the baseballs hitting the canvas backstop with a muted, demoralizing thud.

"Aww . . . lookit that. The little brat's goin' to cry . . ."

He threw the last baseball, sending Bozo down into the water with a loud ka-plunk. Good-natured applause went up from the line behind them waiting for a turn. Sleek and irrepressible as a sewer rat, Bozo scrambled back up on the plank and was quickly unleashing a volley of insults at the woman stepping up to the rail.

"Still high an' dry. Well, lookit this tub of guts!"

They retreated into the crowd.

Theo took in some of his favorite rides, his father trailing along. On the carousel he sat steady in the saddle, if subdued. He got jolted on the bumper cars, yet was cushioned by his own giggles, his mind cleared by the smell of ozone. They climbed aboard a blue Ferris wheel, and reaching the top, their carriage stopped for several minutes as another carriage unloaded below. They swung high above the fairgrounds where one could trace the ten-foot chain-link fence that enclosed its twenty-three acres like a minimum-security prison. The crowd was moving around aimlessly, but acquiring mass. They stared far down Woodward to the south, at the high-rises on the river that looked like a mural against the sky.

"Dad, why did Bozo say those mean things to everybody?"

"Well, that's just his job, Theo. He's trying to insult people and make them so upset they'll want to buy a ticket to try and dunk him. Trouble is that when you're upset you can't throw straight."

"Maybe if he was nice, the people would miss on purpose, to be nice back."

He paused. "That's a neat idea."

Here was his own son's version of the Golden Rule. They watched the traffic flow down Woodward, as if the cars were riding on parallel but invisible rails, their passengers oblivious to the drama of events at the fairgrounds. Each car was a solipsistic bubble, with a separate destination, visual proof of the multiplicity of worlds.

In the livestock area and petting zoo, a 400-pound sow lay like an overturned semi in the straw, nursing a blind swarm of piglets. Baby goats with gleaming pinprick pupils nuzzled grain from Theo's palm, making him squirm with delight. From barred pens, adult sheep and goats stared back at them with moronic intensity. Nearby was another tent, a Birthing Center where three pregnant cows rested on their forelegs in the straw. They were surrounded by a low ring of bleachers where two black women, themselves pregnant, looked on. Doug and Theo took seats near them. Inside the ring an elevated placard announced: Births Due Today. The cows gave no sign of what was pending, gazing back at them with placid resignation.

"Dad, are those cows going to have a baby, like Mom?"

"That's right."

"Don't you think that they should have some privacy?"

"Yes, but it looks like they don't have a choice."

"Well, if you're going to have a baby, you should have a choice."

"That's a smart boy you got there!" spoke up one of the black women next to them. "Yes sir, if a woman gonna have a baby, then she oughta have the right to choose how and where. But that don't happen so much around here.

Instead we end up like cows. It's jus' too bad they don't worship cows in America like they do in India."

He smiled at her, nodding. There was a sense of human kinship in the air. The two women, obviously Detroiters, blended with the dozen or so rural Michiganders seated on the bleachers, most of them white, elderly farmers with strong stooped backs, weathered faces, bodies worn or injured by hard work.

No trace of Bozo's nihilism in this area, only the celebration of birth and growth.

The two of them moved with the crowd: unraveling nuclei of families, clinging teenage couples with brightly dyed hair, kids leaving trails of French fries, popcorn, half-eaten hotdogs, bouquets of cotton candy. Young black men in dew-rags crossed path with suburban white counterparts, decorated with tattoos and piercings. Riders on the near-by Whirligig spun around in an airborne circle with arms raised like the Rapture was upon them.

They bought some hamburgers and Cokes, and then camped on a bench in front of a huge white trailer where a stage protruded from one side. Eight-year-old white girls from the suburbs, wearing taps and sequined dresses, danced to "I'm a Yankee Doodle Dandy." Four teenaged girls from Birmingham in tight shorts performed with hula-hoops, their hips liberated but faces as demure as novitiates in a convent. Black teenage girls from Detroit

offered an epic dance rendition of "Can You Feel It?" –
with big athletic legs, purple costumes, shimmying shoulders, impossibly high kicks. Lying about were restless
kids into horseplay, and solitary men, an old farmer with
a faded baseball cap, a homeless man sleeping in the grass
like a rotting log.

They entered a maze of canvas booths featuring games
of skill. At the radar-timed baseball throw, a uniformed
Vietnam veteran flailed away bravely with a withered right
arm. The shooting gallery was overcrowded, the hunched
backs of men, some dressed in full camouflage, aiming ri-
fles at a moving line of small metal ducks. At a dart throw
booth, Doug broke three balloons to win his son a stuffed
panda, which Theo quickly gave to a toddler who was
vexed and crying at a nearby water fountain, his pizza up-
side-down in the dirt.

The Vietnam War had ended three years ago, but a
mud-brown recruiting trailer was parked near the fence,
where three rock-jawed black Marines in full uniform loitered around a machine gun mounted on a tripod. Theo
was allowed to play around touching the steel barrel of
the weapon. But the trailer was another matter. They had
on display, for a reason that Doug couldn't fathom, an actual electric chair, glowing green in the side bay window.

"Dad, when's Mom coming to meet us?"

"She'll be here in about an hour. Let's walk over in this
direction. I want to check out something."

On the south side of the fairgrounds was a midway and the freak shows. Objections to them had appeared all week in the *Detroit Free Press*, just as protests had arisen two months ago when it was reported that dwarfs were being used as bowling balls at a nearby alley in Royal Oak. The dwarfs challenged the protesters, complaining they were being denied a livelihood. Doug had led his life exploring the wrong side of the tracks, and needed to know which shows had survived this year. Of course, no more bearded ladies, hermaphrodites, legless torsos, geeks, Siamese twins – images from a defunct carnie culture, almost innocent in its mindless cruelty. Still, who were the contemporary freaks?

They cut around canvas booths, past the Haunted House, the Castle of Doom, until they stood before a large round tent, maybe ten yards in diameter, with flap openings on either side. A carnie in a red checkered jacket and bow tie stood selling tickets under a banner reading in brown script: See Konga, The Ape Girl! Inside, the air was hot and humid; the smell of dirt was pungent. A dozen people, mostly black, stood in the half-dark before an elevated wooden stage in the back. On the lip of the stage stood a honey-skinned black girl in a tawny bikini – gorgeous, composed, smiling at the crowd, saying nothing. Soon the man in the checkered jacket closed the flap and joined her on the stage, clutching a small microphone.

"Folks," he said, "you are going to bear witness today to one of the great miracles of life! I'm talking about the theory of evolution itself! That's right, what took thousands of years to happen will take place in the span of an instant right on this stage!" He turned to the girl, an image of innocence despite her bikini. "Folks, please meet Konga! Konga is an African princess captured near Nairobi in the depths of the jungle! The heart of darkness itself! In a moment, you will see her transformed back into the 400-pound body of her ancestor, and it will happen before your eyes!" With befitting gravity, he pulled back a canvas curtain at the back of the stage to reveal a barred cell with a ludicrously big lock on the door. "Folks, because this transformation will take her back in time to a world of darkest evil, we will have to place Konga in this cell, just for your protection. Remember, this is an experiment, and experiments can go wrong. God forbid, if anything *does* go wrong, notice the exit flaps on the two sides of the tent."

He then led the girl into the cell where she sat expressionless on a stool under glaring ceiling lights hidden from view by a black ruffle. He locked the cell door and returned to the lip of the stage, his back to the onlookers, still facing the girl. "Now Konga," he said, his voice rising, "think! Think back! Think back to your roots! Think back to Africa! Think back to your ancestors!"

Bright flashing lights flooded the cell, illuminating the girl who sat staring ahead, trance-like. Then gasps went up from the crowd as a fringe of black fur began to grow over her body, along her forearms, down her bare legs, around the crown of her head, then encircling her face: an absolutely clean illusion. There was an abrupt, explosive noise and smoke. Konga was gone and inside the cell now was a huge gorilla, stomping mad, violently shaking the bars. People all around started to jostle and scream. Then the gorilla tore open the door of his cell, *was loose*, and grappling with the man in the checkered jacket. Pandemonium reigned when both of them rolled off the lip of the stage right at the feet of the crowd and began wrestling furiously in the dirt. "Dad, I want to go," Theo whimpered, and they were carried by the rush of people through the exit flap in the tent. Suddenly all of them were back in the glare of sunlight, the smells of the fairgrounds.

"It's okay, kiddo, it's okay. That was just a trick with mirrors. The girl just switched places with a guy in a gorilla suit. Your dad once had a girlfriend in California with a job like that."

"I don't want to see any more shows . . . I don't want to see Konga any more."

As they wandered away, the man in the red-checkered jacket was back out in front of his tent, looking dapper again, selling tickets for the next show.

Doug's curiosity wasn't yet satisfied. They walked down an alley and by another small, stained tent with a sign:

Pedro: The World's Fattest Man! Beyond the railing was a bale of hay scattered across the dirt, and on a long low bench sat a Hispanic man perspiring profusely, a melting mountain. He must have weighed a quarter ton, though a cardboard sign taped to the tent pole claimed nine hundred pounds. No glitter, no illusion here, just suffering flesh. On another bench behind Pedro sat a tiny brown woman and a small black-eyed boy in a tattered yellow T-shirt, who smiled wanly back at Theo.

"How's it going?"

"Hot, amigo, hot. Too hot today, yes?"

"Business isn't so good?"

"No, no business this year. They put the crazy man with snake right across from me. Nobody want to stop and see me try to cool off."

Pedro's stomach reached out in front of him like two inner tubes balanced on top of each other, above and below a buried belly button. He reached down and grabbed the upper level and hurled it upward like a pizza crust, which allowed air to invade the crevice and offer him some relief.

"Theo, want to go check out the snake guy?"

"No, Dad. I'll play with him." He pointed to the boy in the rear of the tent, then bent under the railing and scampered back.

"Is that okay?"

Pedro nodded.

"Be right back, kiddo. Now do not leave this tent."

Doug moved across the way to a large white trailer with steps leading up to doors at either end. A red sash hung across the front, brandishing in yellow script: Snake Man, Convicted Killer! Selling tickets was a snub-nosed teenager with a shaved head, the orange sleeves of his T-shirt rolled up, revealing a scar running from the top of his shoulder down through a tattoo of a Confederate flag with crossed swords on his bicep. The atmosphere inside the trailer was cramped and airless, white medicinal walls, with just enough room for people to pass single file by a barrier of thick transparent plastic, like those in Detroit convenience stores to protect Chaldean owners from being shot during holdups. Behind the barrier sat a thin, muscular, barebacked kid, maybe twenty, with long, oily locks of blond hair. His skin was so pale it seemed to gleam. Two rattlesnakes were wrapped around his jeans at the waist, their heads bobbing at his chest, tongues flicking out. "What are you starin' at, you jigaboos? Com'on, step inside here an' I'll give you some of this!" And in a kind of spasm, he picked up a short black whip and struck at the barrier that separated him from those in line.

A well-dressed black couple in front of Doug hesitated. They looked like they had come straight from church. The woman in her yellow chiffon dress wanted to retreat, but there was no way once in line to back out. Everyone had to file by the Snake Man, who looked deranged, perhaps on glue or meth, daring any set of eyes to engage his own. Racist rant flickered from his mouth like an invisible flame: "You niggers done with yur rioting today? Takin' yur swarm of kids down to the welfare office, are ya? I hate all you fuckin' jungle bunnies!"

For a moment Doug stood right in front of the Snake Man. That composure was cold as ice. This was not part of any show; the circumstances gave him complete freedom to lash out with impunity. Behind Doug, two young blacks in Piston jerseys glared at him, but restrained by the barrier, could only pass on and out. In front of him, the woman in the chiffon dress was crying as she left the trailer, inching down the steps back into the crowd.

He wanted to reach out to her, apologize for his race, but she was gone. Instead he reclaimed his son from the World's Fattest Man, and the two of them headed back toward the middle of the fairgrounds.

"How was the snake man, Dad?"

He felt a queasy, voyeuristic complicity in the shows he had been so eager to seek out. "He was mean. I'm glad you didn't see it."

"Let's go find Mom now."

"Sure. We're supposed to meet her over where the wrestling tournament will be, near where Bozo was."

"I don't want to see him any more either."

Elizabeth was waiting near the flagpole, which rose up beside an elevated boxing ring draped in red-white-and-blue crepe paper. Her beauty made her stand out from the crowd: thick black hair, skin the color of cream, striking hazel eyes. She hugged Theo, and then said with vexation, "I've been waiting for you two for half an hour." They'd been quarreling lately, so Doug was surprised when she turned suddenly and gave him a lascivious kiss, then placed her head on his shoulder.

They stuck around to catch the Battle Royal – a dozen semi-professional wrestlers and other toughs competing for $50,000, the winner the last one in the ring. But it was such mayhem up there, so many limbs to twist, faces to smack, that they were almost paralyzed, locked in a fraternal, slow-motion waltz: a grunting, sweating wad of flesh. Two beer-bellied white men were pushing next to Doug, screeching at the fake violence in a psychotic suspension of disbelief. He needed no more revelations of national character. The last wrestler in the ring was a burly black behemoth that introduced himself as Junk Yard Dog when he received his check. "How's I gonna pay the taxes on this thing?" he lamented to the crowd with a wink.

But by now Elizabeth and Theo were already heading for the exit gate on Woodward Avenue. As he ran to catch up, a familiar refrain reached his ears, one aimed directly at him.

"Lookit this poor guy. Gotta face like a donkey, don't he? . . . Com'on, Hee-Haw, throw it!"

The Blue Pearl

I stood in front of a large, yellow, wood-framed house on the western edge of downtown Chicago. This was the Zen temple where three days of meditation, called a *sesshin*, were about to start.

I had arrived that afternoon from Detroit on Amtrak. Not prepared for the physical ordeal ahead, I limbered up by sitting on my calves in the seat of the rumbling coach, jacket thrown over his thighs, staring out the window at rolling Michigan farmland spotted with snowdrifts like white burial mounds. A conductor walking down the aisle mistook me for an amputee and offered a bottle of water. "No thanks," I replied. "I'm just in pursuit of the Blue Pearl."

Now, I climbed the stairs to the roshi's apartment on the second floor.

Inside the door stood a short, compactly built man with a full head of black hair that was shaved to the skull. A mailman by day, which I knew from a previous visit, he had eyes as wide as pizzas. Another arrival, a young woman, slipped by me and gave the roshi a tiny trumpet from

Tibet and some saint's bones in a vial. He accepted these absurd offerings graciously, which impressed me.

Soon I stood in the next room, beside a monk watching local TV news. A collision and derailment had occurred on the "L" an hour ago. Several passengers were reported dead, and images of paramedics removing bloodied bodies from twisted coaches flashed on the screen.

I'd been on those tracks about that time and place. Word circulated that the roshi's wife had been on that same "L" line and was still not accounted for. He would carry this awareness inside him all evening, without a sign of anxiety or concern. He was a rock.

Zen teaches you life hangs by a thread.

And then there is the Blue Pearl – a tiny light of cobalt blue that can appear during meditation. According to Zen masters, it's the subtlest covering of the individual soul, capable of expanding and totally enveloping a person. Always the color of the open sky and the largest of living creatures, the blue whale. The jewel of enlightenment.

All of us left the apartment and went downstairs into a meditation hall or zendo. Soon maybe thirty people were milling around there, a mix of students, white-collar professionals, normal middle-class types, longhairs, bohemians, young and old. Chants followed, a chime rang, and the *sesshin* started.

We took cushions and assumed full or half-lotus

positions, facing one of the four walls. Then a gong vibrated and everyone meditated for forty minutes. It's a long time to be staring at a blank wall, fighting off mental panic and physical pain. We rose for *kinhin,* a slow, dignified walk in single file around the zendo, then back onto the cushions for another forty minutes of meditation. I struggled mightily, fighting off drowsiness, stabbing pain in my legs. Someone's foot next to mine started shaking frenetically.

It wasn't yet time to pursue the Blue Pearl. Better to just let the mind settle as best it could into a receptive emptiness.

I was still recovering from my spiritual mentor back in Detroit. A black barber named Otis, a black belt in karate who'd had me out punching the trunks of trees. He said there's a karate master on Okinawa who could punch out charging bulls. What he did first was smash his knuckles with a sledgehammer, then rearrange them into a flat, more potent hitting surface. But ever punch a tree? It is *hard.* For months my knuckles were purple, scabbed, gruesomely swollen. Overall my hands looked like psychedelic mittens. Why continue this? No more Otis.

Before that there was Baba. An Indian guru I'd met under a white tent filled with devotes high in the Catskills. He was seated on a raised wooden platform, handsome and brown-skinned, wearing a knit cap and red toga. His toes were wiggling and seemed to glow. When the service was over, people came forward to give Baba a gift, I had no gift, but luckily a hippie, looking like he could get lost in the color blue forever, slipped me a grapefruit. I walked down the aisle and knelt before Baba and gave him the grapefruit. He stood up, towering above me, and hit me across the head with a bouquet of peacock feathers. At that instant I experienced *shaktipat*. A white H-bomb went off in my head. My organs and muscles began to shake at the base of my spine, and my mind, hitherto skeptical and overly critical, was now reeling in an ecstasy that would reduce an orgasm to lacing your shoes. But who could embrace a spiritual mentor linked to Oakland's criminal underworld who sexually abused his teenage devotees? No more Baba.

My hands looked normal now, resting on my thighs, forming a circle with thumb and index fingers. I became gradually aware of the defrocked monk, sitting three cushions down, who had been so kind to me last summer. Alan was no longer wearing his yellow robe, and kept raising his arms over his head to signal for the *kyosaku,* a stick used to strike your shoulders during meditation to sharpen concentration. Indeed, another monk whacked the hell out of him all evening long. Was there some kind of punishment or penance going on?

But punishment violates the spirit of Zen.

As for my own meditation, I got nowhere. *Makyo,* or illusion, filled my head. The day's residue floated up like trash along a curb. No distant watery horizons came into view. No trace of the Blue Pearl.

Rather I was mired in hateful thoughts of Kathlene, now contesting me in Detroit courts for custody of our son and daughter. I imagined her miraculously removed from my life by some catastrophic accident. I daydreamed of sudden omniscience, of knowing *everything* there is to know about life, leaving me unable to speak, and subsequently locked in an Alzheimer's ward where people had come to know nothing at all. Not a very Zen-like state, and I pulled out of it by imagining the roshi's wife trapped in a twisted coach.

As we repeated cycles of meditation, rising for *kinhin* became harder, my legs asleep or stilts of pain. Once I came close to stumbling into the roshi. Others circling the zendo were sneezing, farting loudly, some doubled up with muffled laughter. There was no harmony to any of this. I wanted to be somewhere else. By the fourth sitting I was in such pain that my vision failed, the wall became sheer fuzziness. No surface cracks, no chipped paint to cling to, get lost in, no way to pass spiritually beyond the wall.

The meditation was over by eleven o'clock, and I slipped out of the temple and walked up the street in freezing darkness to a diner. The defrocked monk was there. I joined him at the counter and ordered hot chocolate.

We exchanged pleasantries, and then I asked, "Alan, is there any word about the roshi's wife?"

"She's safe," he replied. "Apparently stayed downtown

with a friend."

We were quiet a moment, the cup warm in my hand.

"You're calling for the *kyosaku* a lot," I said. "Any reason for that?"

"Sitting is power," he said, without conviction. "That's all there is to it. Potentially we have propellers growing out of our heads . . ."

"We do?"

"Yes. Strong thrusts of spirit. The stick can get them turning. It can also punish. You know, I edit the temple's newsletter, and last week I carelessly misspelled schizo-phrenia as 'S-K-I-T-S-ophrenia' in an article. The roshi is still angry."

I looked at him.

"But Alan, anger is not Zen, but exactly what it aims to overcome. I hope you can help the roshi with his prob-lem . . . But tomorrow I'm going for the Blue Pearl." Just speaking this way, as if competing for a trophy, should have warned me, but it didn't.

Soon we walked back to the temple and found everyone laid out wall to wall in sleeping bags on the floor of the zendo. I had a dream that night of searching in the dark for the bathroom only to step on the roshi's head.

Everyone was awakened by 4:45 a.m. We sipped some tea, and then went back to meditation. My efforts were clean-er, but still shallow, without resolve. There were fleeting daydreams, memories of my father taking me to the Polo Grounds in NYC, of playing rugby against a team of Welsh coalminers in Cardiff, then floating afterwards in the mud-darkened common bath of an ancient locker room.

This was not helpful. Memory had to be played over and over on the wall, overexposed as it were, and converted to blank film. To ever reach the Blue Pearl, I needed some help from the *kyosaku*. I raised my arms, and a monk laid four whacks on my shoulders that knocked the spots I was staring at off the wall.

Then the Blue Pearl appeared.

As if from another realm, a blue gem on the wall, in three dimensions, the sparkling light casting a glow of infinite generosity and compassion. I wanted to enter that zone, but knew almost instantly that I could not. Aspiration faltered. I liked my own self well enough to be reluctant to cash it in. Besides, I could never match the Buddhist monks I respected, like those in the streets of Saigon, setting themselves on fire to protest the war. Wrapped in flames, they never broke their posture before collapsing into ashes.

Maybe I preferred the usual personal fuckups to being rescued by Zen.

Though Zen's generosity gave space for the individual to bloom, reality was bigger than anyone's own imaginings. My allegiance remained with those not enlightened. Soon enough the Blue Pearl started to fade from the orange sunlit wall like a lantern losing kerosene. I tried to bring it back, only to find myself staring at a giant bottle of milk suspended right before my nose. But hallucinations don't count.

By the close of the fourth sitting, my legs were in such agony I just broke posture and thrust them straight out toward the wall. It brought instant, delirious relief. Fuck this. Zen had to grant one the wisdom of accepting a bad day. Something did come from nothing. I thought of Pascal, saying all our woes stem from an inability to sit quietly in a room alone.

But I needed some Western woes by now, just to balance the view. So I walked out of the temple at noon into dazzling winter sunlight. All that meditation, however impure, had left my mind very lucid. I had an almost hallucinatory take on physical objects: traffic light, car fenders, sandwich board, dog pooping. I was touched to learn later that the roshi had asked about my absence.

I spent the afternoon at the Lincoln Park zoo, and while walking through the new gorilla exhibit, was set upon by a huge silverback that suddenly charged the glass wall, banging his head trying to get at me. It shook me up. Gorillas should know I loved them.

That night I went off to a disco club on Rush Street, alive with mirrors, glass ball, loud music, and bare flesh. An hour in the haze of strobe lights turned those of us on the dance floor into flickering shadows, like actors in a silent movie. I decided I loved Chicago. I drank at the bar with a pretty brunette who walked dogs for a living, holding a dozen leashes in her hands marching down Michigan Avenue. I told her about the vet living on my block in Detroit who treated dogs whose owners had cut out their tongues to keep them from barking. There was a nerdy hedge fund manager with an orange bow tie, bragging about his Wall Street thefts. Then a green-eyed woman with stringy red hair was hanging around me, whispering she wanted to get fucked tonight, somewhere, by somebody.

At one point I tried to pass into the "Members Only" section of the club, but was blocked by a gorgeous young woman in full usher's uniform. "Are you from the public bar?" she asked.

"Yes, my dear, but didn't you start there yourself?"

The green-eyed woman came up behind me. "Don't worry about this one," she said sarcastically. "He thinks he's enlightened."

The next morning I rode Amtrak back to Detroit.

The sesshin wasn't quite the end of Zen for me. I meditated now and then just to stay composed, keep my mind laundered. Concentrating on the act of breathing in silent stillness always seemed to deliver some latent strength.

But there was no need to worry about its ultimate success. Losing my son and daughter in the custody fight would pull me back into *dukkha,* the world of suffering, for the long haul. The Blue Pearl was gone for good, but then that jewel must have been rejected by Buddhists I most admired, the bodhisattvas, the compassionate ones who turn away from nirvana to deal with people like me.

Sports Arenas

The Farmington youth soccer arena was a hockey rink with a green rug instead of ice inside the sideboards. The roof might work for indoor tennis. A game was under way and fathers sat high in the bleachers, exhorting their sons to "Step up!" "Run!" "Don't back off!" "Shoot!" Appeals for aggression within the rules that would demonstrate these twelve-year-olds, at least their own, had the right stuff. The fathers yelled at the referee too, often with calculation. One sitting behind me, who, after swearing up a storm over a call, turned to a friend and chuckled, "I was just working on his next call."

Weary-eyed mothers, many overweight, sat several rows below us under heating lights. Their younger kids were climbing up and down the bleachers. That's not a good sound, people of any age scampering around on aluminum bleachers. The mothers were more mysterious. They watched the game going on beyond the sideboards, but not as spectators to a competition, armed with anger and judgment, not obsessed with outcomes. Instead they were just present, responding either to encourage their sons or to protect them. When one boy went down on the rug, writhing in pain after a flagrant foul, they rose to their feet, in unison, not in protest but rather some primal empathy. They seemed to me the closest thing to sanity in the arena.

Why was I seated in the bleachers? I worked nearby, and years ago did coach the only youth soccer team in Detroit. But why was I showing up in places like this where I didn't belong? It wasn't unpleasant. My sons had left home to pursue their open futures years ago. Maybe it was the pull of nostalgia, or some mid-life immobilization. And yes, I was hooked on espionage, seeking out moments where I actually felt I was witnessing something for the first time. Always ripe for self-deception.

Recently this state of mind had led me into other places where I didn't belong. Last week there was a snow-covered golf course outside of Ann Arbor where I played in the Chili Open, named for the temperature and food promised after the tourney. Six short holes where we tried to strike an orange golf ball inside an orange chalk circle on the green. My first drive duck-hooked into a FedEx truck coming down the road, but the rules allowed an unlimited number of lost balls. I used a five-iron to drive a lot of them into neighboring farmland. In a game that rewarded accuracy and precision, there was something almost euphoric about deliberately hitting a golf ball out of bounds into white snow.

Or watching a night of Golden Gloves boxing matches in the old wooden field house at the State Fairgrounds. My head would flash with epiphanies every time the bell sounded. The sparse, largely black crowd had moved up close to the ring, which stood out like a stage under the floodlights. All evening, voices in the front rows around me offered running commentary: "He don't wanna go in there." "Leroy, you stumped at 'im. Won't work, gotta punch 'im in the belly button." "Mohammad, you got to hit what you see. There ain't nuthin' up there where yur swingin'." "James, yur plug has come out. You got to fight. Hit 'im in the snoot." And there was Sam, yet another black teenager from Detroit. shuffling down the aisle of loose dirt in a purple terrycloth bathrobe, pausing when he reached wooden steps leading up into the ring. "Sam, you walk like you was scared . . . You scared?" He grinned back, revealing gaps of missing teeth. During the referee's instructions, he seemed sacrificial – thin body, arms dangling down to his knees, shoulder blades protruding like stunted wings. He had the genial vacancy of the retarded. His opponent, black and muscular, stood facing him in the middle of the ring, glistening, chewing on a white mouthpiece. When the bell rang Sam moved forward until a hard left jab made him pensive, and then a salvo of heavy punches sent him to the canvas.

Or going to the Motor City Tattoo Expo held at the Renaissance Center in downtown Detroit. The entire third floor was filled with tattoo artists from around the world, with women in revealing, colorful dresses, their lovely breasts, well tattooed, spilling out of loose halters, the men in black leather jackets with studs all over the back and sleeves. Here was another sport, competing for the title of most bizarre. Many had come to be tattooed, which could take ten hours or more, at $100 to $1,000 an hour. They were scattered about, seated on benches, cots, recliners, offering up a bare shoulder, leg, thigh, back, forearm, or neck as a canvas. Artists used automatic needle-machines dipped in dye to deliver the ink into the second layer of skin. It would take lasers to blast the skin cells and allow the ink to be absorbed into the body to remove it. I knew nothing about tattoos, which seemed like buying new clothes you couldn't take off, now inseparable from the body. I didn't own any T-shirt with any writing or design on it, preferring to go unfathomed. But the crowd was interesting, cultish, the tattoos beyond description in their color and delicate elaboration. Animals, plants, monsters, naked women, insects, figures from myth, religion, the zodiac – just about anything you could dream up, made as intricate and arresting as a butterfly wing. I learned that 40% of Americans had at least one emblazoned or hidden on their bodies. When leaving, I asked a Dutch artist why people wanted tattoos. He gazed upward and reflected, "It all begins in woe."

I must have liked not belonging.

The soccer game beyond the sideboards was winding down. A one-goal difference and the fathers were lathered up. The boys out on the rug were highly skilled, yet oddly self-absorbed and workmanlike. They played without passion except when fouled. They exuded an air of indifference, almost boredom, and when the final horn sounded they wandered off the rug with shrugs. To me they looked burned out, as if somehow the competitiveness of their overreaching fathers has snuffed out their own. They were playing soccer, yes, but as one of many games, with real life awaiting them. Perhaps the experience was expanding their minds, pointing them toward some new spiritual frontier beyond competition.

Then I watched a blond-haired kid as he climbed wearily over the sideboards, uniform clinging to his skin, only to be immediately surrounded by three pretty, giggling girls. The sight unburdened me, placing me back where I belonged. It felt good knowing nothing.

Blue Chalk

He was fifty-five, unruly hair flecked with gray, body trim and athletic. He was living alone in Ann Arbor. This morning he was seated in the rear of a downtown coffee house writing in his journal. Yesterday he came upon an armless juggler in red tights staring sadly through a wire fence as kids raced across an empty playground. He wrote that down even though it didn't happen. What he needed was a woman to come forward and claim him for no particular reason. That might make a difference, but he knew it wasn't going to happen at his age. All around him at other tables were students and young professionals, their laptops open, eyes riveted on the brightly colored screens.

At the front windows a bearded man abandoned his laptop, stood up, and started reading aloud from *The New York Times*. The self-appointed oracle drew stares and irked expressions. A toaster popped up somewhere, a burst of laughter. Two teenage girls in tight blue-jeans and pink sneakers stood at the counter nearby, ordering lattes and talking loudly about the free condoms now available at their high school. Suddenly beams of sunlight poured through the front windows, creating a musty glow. But no dream of deliverance was going to spring to life in this coffee house for him. Everyone in here might as well be going "beep-beep."

He slid the journal into a knapsack and reached for his jacket.

"Don't go. Please, stay for a minute."

He looked up at a woman in a loose calico dress standing near the table. She was a little overweight, but attractive, even voluptuous. Her blue eyes and pixie haircut appealed to him, and for a moment he felt incapable of linear thought.

"Hello. Would you like to sit down?"

She did, and then immediately began speaking, her voice soft, confidential, almost conspiratorial. "I can tell you don't recognize me, but we've met, years ago. We were eleven or twelve in Independence, Missouri. Your family had just moved in from somewhere in New Jersey, and I had a terrible crush on you. I used to follow you around and would spy on you when you and your pals hung out on that grassy train trestle at the edge of our neighborhood. You would wait for the train to come through, balanced on the tracks, and leap off at the last minute. Then all of you would wait in the grass until the caboose came by and a railroad man would stand at the back rail and throw you sticks of thick colored chalk. I think they were used to mark up the boxcars."

The voice reached him, fragments of memory floating back.

"I remember that day at school you walked up without a word and gave me a blue piece of railroad chalk. That made my heart pound because I realized you were aware of me watching you on the tracks. I was so in love, yet had no way to show you. The next week you guys weren't playing on the trestle, but across the tracks in the far woods. You had BB guns, had divided into two sides and were shooting at each other, playing war games I guess. I waited for you on the tracks. I was desperate for some way to thank you for the chalk. Then a train whistle sounded in the distance. In a kind of dream I lay down between the rails and pressed into the gravel. I had heard you guys say that if you squeezed up small enough, and stayed real still, a train would pass right over without touching you. The whistle hooted louder and closer, and I just shut my eyes . . . Suddenly you were pulling us down the side of the trestle as the train rumbled by. We lay in the grass beside each other for a long while. You looked at me in wonder. Then you said, 'Don't try that again.' I remember the welt on your cheek, maybe from a BB. 'That chalk was just an extra piece,' you added as you stood up and went off to find your pals. And I never did pursue you again. Your family soon moved again anyway. So when I walked into the coffee shop this morning and saw you, made sure it was you, I wanted to thank you for saving my life."

He stared at her and frowned. He didn't remember any of this story. She may as well have arrived from the same realm as the armless juggler. Yet that wasn't true. He did remember the train trestle in Independence, the railroad chalk thrown to him and his buddies from the caboose, the war games and BB guns in the woods. But how could this woman know any of these details unless she was there, unless her story was true? She was attractive; there was no doubt about that. Could there be a hole in his memory? Were there other critical parts of his life that were not remembered?

He stretched out his arms above his head in a gesture of dreamy calculation. "Well," he said, "perhaps you could save mine now."

Before the Surgery

I walked down the hill with my two Labs into a green meadow. The sun shone down from a brainless blue sky. I limped because it hurt to walk, usually the simplest thing you can do. I was going to have surgery in a week to replace my hip. They do this surgery a thousand times a day. They'll give me a local anesthetic, a shot low in the spinal cord called an epidural. The same shot they give to women giving birth. You might say I will be born again with a metal hip joint. I'll be conscious throughout as the doctors cut into my thigh, saw off the part of my femur that forms a ball at the top, then drive a titanium spike into the femur with a metal ball on top, then punch a metal socket into my pelvic bone, then snap the ball into the socket like a tinker toy and sew me back up. It's a crude, bloody procedure that you might expect to see in a slaughterhouse. I'll hear all the noises, the saw, hammer, and the rest. I won't witness the surgery because they'll place a little cloth fence across my abdomen to block the view. With luck I will be walking around with no pain in a few months. The miracle of modern medicine. I stopped halfway across the meadow to ease the pain and pull some pieces of raw hot dog from my pocket to feed the Labs. I paused to watch two teenage boys maybe twenty yards away playing keep-away soccer. Their footwork and fluidity were miraculous, springing up from falls as if born to run. The Labs abandoned me to join the boys in the rites of soccer, a game I excelled at in college years ago.

That morning I had searched two envelopes of family photos to get some new images and tape them on the refrigerator to greet my sister when she arrived to assist me after the surgery. In most of the photos I am in my thirties and forties, a very good-looking guy. I'm sixty-two now, not so good-looking, face weary and lined, bushy hair thinning noticeably. I don't think there's any surgery to halt the aging process. It's just a question of patch, patch, patch as my father used to say when he was alive and still tied to a dying animal. Yes, I'll be moving a lot better in two to three months, but after all, only moving faster toward death. Maybe something will go wrong and I'll not make it through surgery. That happens. Everyone knows that hospitals kill thousands of patients each year.

In excruciating pain I limped up the hill with the Labs and the three of us walked to the car. On the sidewalk we passed a small girl, maybe eleven, with blue eyes and pigtails, whirling a red hula-hoop around her hips. It leveled out and rose slightly like a plastic halo that promised never to waver or fall.

Ian and Poppa

His grandson was three years old and tall for his age. Visiting for a week, he would catch himself staring at him, the tawny hair, blue eyes and full red lips. Yes, a handsome lad, but so far he had paid no attention to Poppa. Twin siblings had arrived since his last visit, so Ian had larger matters on his mind. Why was he was no longer the exclusive focus of his parents' devotion? Walking to the Safeway Market yesterday, when he asked him what he wanted for dinner, the boy quipped, "We could eat the babies."

His son was aware of all this, smiling wearily. Mike and Anna were up every two hours throughout the night.

Ian rejected any of his offers to play soccer in the back yard or read a book together, preferring his parents' company. That was fine, but the rudeness, walking away without any no-thank-you or even acknowledgement of his existence irked Poppa. But so be it. Who could understand a three-year-old? He decided to step back and ignore him, or at least pretend to. Wasn't there a lesson to be learned here about rudeness and its consequences?

Things between the two of them did warm up by

midweek. At least they related. When he and Ian were in the back yard, Poppa wanted to teach him how to take a level swing with a whiffle bat and hit a plastic baseball off a tee. After all, what other kid had a grandfather who had been offered a minor league contract from the Detroit Tigers? Not that Ian should care. He was too disturbed by his fancied abandonment, too committed to a willful, reactive independence to be coachable at the moment. Instead he preferred to attack the hitting tee, jumping up and down on its base, insisting it was a pogo stick.

One day Poppa went to pick him up from preschool with his daughter-in-law. These were magical places in university towns. Filled with bright colors and wholesome activities designed to build self-esteem and teach good citizenship. In his youth, Poppa had just roamed neighborhoods with his friends, exploring the bulldozed basements of new houses, scaling their wooden scaffolding, climbing tall trees to the top, digging secret dugouts in vacant lots, playing endless games of mumblety-peg with pocketknives on green grass. Hours, afternoons, days of freedom with no parents around, when anything goes and life had a sweet sense of danger.

Poppa was far from there now, catching his reflection in the mirror of a closet bathroom for the school kids. He tried to avoid his reflection at all times, but it would happen, or he would be caught in photos or videos. He honestly didn't recognize the face now, the wrinkles, the haggardness, the wincing gaze, and the gray hair scruffy and thinning. Then he spied Ian napping on a blanket in a hallway, and woke him up. The boy blinked, rubbed his eyes, and then jumped up and raced to get something he had drawn for Poppa earlier in the day. There were stars on blue paper, inside a mysterious constellation of wiggly lines.

The last night of his visit, he watched Mike lead Ian into the bedroom to put him down. He could overhear his son reading books, talking softly, nudging his son toward sleep. But an hour later he came back out defeated, saying, "Poppa, it's your turn. Ian wants you in there."

He was delighted – even though his son warned him the boy knew all the tricks of the trade. "He'll suddenly say, I have to pee, and he usually does. Then he'll say, Daddy, I have to pooh. We're potty-training him, so we have to let him try, even though we know he's stalling. He can't quit on the day, especially just when he finally has his parents to himself without the twins around. He just took a big pooh, but I swear the little bugger always saves a little something for later if needed."

Poppa walked into Ian's bedroom. It was dark, except for an illuminated green turtle on the carpet that project-ed stars and a quarter moon on the ceiling and walls. He sat on the floor beside the bed, and started telling stories he had told Mike at that age. It was an old valise of mem-ories, mostly improvisations on *Gulliver's Travels,* where the shipwrecked Englishman has many adventures on unknown islands. Ian liked how Gulliver saved the tiny capitol of the Lilliputians from going up in flames by peeing on the city, or how he escaped from being roasted by a tribe of cannibals with the help of orangutans playing violins. They took turns singing songs, Poppa with "Old Man River," Way Down Upon the Sewanee River," "Jubilation T. Cornpone," and "Trouble Right Here in River City." Ian had his own favorites, "Twinkle Twinkle Little Star" and others.

But after an hour the boy seemed more awake than when his grandfather came in.

"Ian, it's time to get to sleep."

"Poppa, I have to go pooh."

"Your dad said you just did."

"I have to go pooh again."

In the bathroom, he sat on the rim of the tub across from Ian on his little potty. Could he actually summon some more pooh? He looked at Poppa, sensing the challenge. His face grew concentrated and turned pink with exertion, then a sudden sigh of relief. Checking down between his legs, Ian looked up at him with a triumphant smile.

"Plunk," he said.

"Nice going. If I did that it might be an accident."

The boy thought about that remark, then gave up and had to assume that his grandfather might have some wisdom. Just not transmissible, beyond his reach, meaningless.

Demolition

Jake is seventy-four. Watching him lower himself from a standing position to the floor is like watching the slow-motion demolition of a building. He bends forward, his knees buckle, and one palm reaches down to the floor, then the other, then down on one knee, then the other. And by God he is on all fours! When eighteen he may have crawled through thick jungle or elephant grass in Vietnam, returning from his LP post to the platoon of Marines in the Au Shau Valley. Or a decade later he might have been back on his knees, playing a bucking bronco in the living room with the legs of his young son clinging to his waist to fight being thrown off. But that was all history. Now he can just crawl across the floor, perhaps through that doorway, perhaps into another room. Certainly not into another world, like the wars in Iraq and Afghanistan he covered as a journalist twenty years ago, or the women he knew in foreign lands. Now back on his knees, there is no option but to go all the way down, if only to avoid the indignity of scuttling across the floor like some beached crab seeking the shoreline. With aging, his pride has given way, by and large, to a playfully ironic attempt to avoid humiliation.

With an arm as support, Jake lowers his left hip to the floor, releasing its weight, then the other hip goes down, and he stretches his legs out as far as they will go. What a relief it is to be just sitting on the floor! Rather like that scraggly, bearded panhandler on the sidewalk that he walked by yesterday, dropping a dollar bill into his navy cap. Yet the relief is only temporary, because he is still leaning on arms that are locked straight behind him, palms down, like the back of a chair, not a posture comfortable for long.

But his demolition is not complete. Planting a left elbow on the floor, he leans sideways and rolls onto his back, then slowly lowers his head until he is lying flat on the floor, legs straight out, arms limp and angled slightly away from his body. How relaxing this position is, like he is floating on air! Not unlike the mescaline trips he took on the beaches of Monterrey years ago, or the anesthesia taking hold before his heart bypass last year. Except this feeling is better. He can press his palms flat to the floor and feel no pressure, mere drift. He is down entirely at last, eyes staring up at the ceiling, a new surface to attract his attention, surprisingly not as high from this vantage. Soon his eyes may close, close slowly, and he will feel at peace.

And now I ask you – who knows how to resurrect a demolished building? You can't even find the old bricks, mortar, plaster, or wood in the wreckage. Even the steel girders are bent. Everything is unrecognizable or turned to dust, irreversibly. But no dynamite expertly placed at critical junctures in the building was used in the case of Jake. The causes of his demolition are internal – stenosis, arthritis, diabetes, coronary disease, hip replacement, the list goes on. Of course, just about anyone his age could compile such a list of physical ailments, and in fact he is among the lucky ones. He is still alive. He has participated in or witnessed the crucial events of his generation. He has given to the world two remarkable sons. His writings comprise a small, but relevant part of the historical record.

Could there perhaps be hope for his resurrection where there isn't for a building? Can he find new sinews, bones, heart, nerves, and fingernails? And if so, could they be woven into the miracle of a human body? Could he elude mortality and stay among us? But no, that is not likely. Perhaps in an afterlife, but it is rumored only spirit exists there. Besides, he believes in neither stick nor stone. Plus, after seventy-four years, gravity is pushing down on him in earnest. A force he didn't acknowledge much in his lifetime, it is now determined to push him not just to the floor, but through it into the earth itself.

Jake lies there on the floor. Demolished. Hadn't he better try to get up immediately before it is too late?

ACKNOWLEGEMENT

Grateful acknowledgement is made to the following publications where stories in this collection first appeared, at times in different form and with different titles:

The Gettysburg Review: "Freaks"

The Antioch Review: "Wrecks"

Crazyhorse: "Mr. Gullick"

The Iowa Review: "Meat Squad," "Black Lava"

Boulevard: "Angling With My Father," "Her," "Listening," "Before the Surgery"

Chicago Quarterly Review: "The Diplomat," "Bus Ride," "Underdog"

Aethlon: "The Pinch Hitter," "Luxury Suite"

North American Review: "Blue Chalk"

The Chariton Review: "Sailing"

Witness: "B. J."

The New York Times: "Out-of-Work Line"

Broad Street: "The Blue Pearl"

34th Parallel: "Memorial," "The Party," "Demolition"

The Saint Ann's Review: "Hereafter"

CPSIA information can be obtained
at www.ICGtesting.com
Printed in the USA
JSHW020822080919
1382JS00003B/5